THE GIRL WITH THE IRON TOUCH

Also available from Kady Cross
and
Harlequin TEEN

The Steampunk Chronicles series in reading sequence:

THE GIRL WITH THE IRON TOUCH

Kady Cross

HARLEQUIN® TEEN

ISBN-13: 978-0-373-21085-5

THE GIRL WITH THE IRON TOUCH

Printed in U.S.A.

For Jess Lanigan, who has hand-sold this series, talked it up
to anyone who will listen, and makes me feel like a superstar.
Thank you for your incredible enthusiasm, and for reminding me
what it feels like when the future is full of nothing but promise.
You break my heart, girl, and I love you to bits.

For TS, probably the sweetest—and tallest—editor I've ever had.
Thank you for getting behind this series, and thank you to
everyone at Harlequin TEEN (Natashya, Lisa, Mary)
for being so fabulous to work with.

For Miriam, my agent and my friend who believes in me
no matter what. You rock, my dear.

This book is also for Steve, because he lets me sing when we
play Rock Band, never blinks when I dye my hair or asks me,
"Are you really going out in that?" A long time ago I made a wish,
and then you came true. Thanks, babe.

Chapter 1

London, Autumn, 1897

A giant tentacle slapped the front of the submers
ible, driving the small craft backward in the water. A
crack no wider than a hair split across the view screen
as suckers the size of dinner plates pulled free.

"Mary and Joseph," Emily O'Brien muttered as
murky water from the Thames began to seep in through
that crack. A sound like breaking ice followed as pressure from the outside pushed against the glass, demand
ing to get inside like a rowdy drunkard at a tavern door.

"Goin' up!" she yelled. "The control room's been

breached!" She shoved hard on the guiding lever, forcing the vehicle to rise quickly.

The crack grew.

Emily held her breath.

The glass popped—another crack shot downward.

She should have covered the glass with a protective
metal grid.

Water spilled onto the control panel. Sparks flew.
Emily pulled her goggles down over her eyes and
shoved against the lever, as though she could make the
craft move faster with sheer force of will.

Well, actually she could probably do just that.

Water ran onto her boots. The glass was a spiderweb
of cracks. Any second the entire thing would burst inward, cutting her to ribbons before she drowned.

Her jaw set stubbornly. Fear was for the weak. "This
is *not* my day to die!" She tore off her gloves and set her
bare hands against the sub's control panel. She took a
deep breath, ignored the tiny trickles of icy water that
ran beneath her palms and *commanded* the craft to rise.
The mechanized workings of the craft recognized the
order and jumped to do her bidding.

The sub shot upward so quickly she lost her footing,
landing hard on the wet floor. Daylight flooded the
cabin as the glass shattered. Daylight, not water.

"Emily!" cried a voice in her ear. "Em!"

"I'm all right," she replied. Later she'd smile over the worry in Sam's voice. With the amount of time she'd spent worrying over him, it was nice to have the tables turned.

Her enjoyment was brief. She rose up on her hands and knees only to slip on the wet metal beneath her boots. Pain exploded in her chest as she hit the metal floor. A tentacle as thick as her waist whipped the air where her head had been not two seconds earlier as she rolled to her back. Suckers attached to the ceiling and pulled. The submersible's nose pitched down, cold, pungent water spilling inside the jagged hole left by the shattered glass.

Emily grabbed hold of the foot of the ladder to keep from tumbling through that hole. Her chest hurt from the fall, and from her heart pounding against her ribs. Were they broken or just bruised? Would one pierce her lung?

It wouldn't matter if the beastie pulling her under the water succeeded in killing and probably devouring her. She'd take her chances on a punctured lung.

Cold, dirty water sloshed over the tops of her boots and soaked through her woolen trousers as she pulled herself to her knees. Clinging to the ladder, she rose to her feet and began to climb. Her sodden clothes and sloshing boots worked against her, keeping her movements slow and awkward.

She turned the wheel on the ceiling hatch, arms straining as she pushed against it. The Thames rushed into the craft over the jagged opening in the front of the craft. She had but seconds before it was completely pulled under. A tentacle brushed her leg. She shuddered, heart racing. Emily put all of her strength into opening the hatch, ignoring the burning in her chest and arms.

The lock disengaged with a thunk. She pushed the hatch open and scampered up the ladder as the tentacle reached for her once more. The rubbery flesh looped around her boot, but she yanked her leg up before it closed around her leg like a vice. She climbed onto the top of the submersible and slammed the hatch on the slick, gray appendage, amputating the tip. It slid away, leaving a bloody trail.

A roar escaped from the water. Emily looked up in time to see the Kraken rise out of the river. And though it had been a long time since she'd been to church, or even believed in God, she crossed herself.

"Emily!"

It was Sam. He stood on the dock, the helmet off his underwater suit, a look of absolute terror on his rugged face. It was that look that decided her fate. She was not going to let him see her die. He might be physically the strongest person in the world, but inside he was as soft as a puppy.

And she loved him for it.

So Emily ran. The submersible shook as another tentacle hit—the Kraken was coming for her. She almost slipped but kept moving. Her fingers fumbled at her belt, pulled the gun strapped there free of its holster. She aimed it at a point just above Sam's head—the building behind him—and pulled the trigger.

A thin rope with a claw attachment on the end shot from the gun and latched on to the wooden building. Emily wrapped both hands around the pistol and pulled the trigger again. She was yanked off her feet just as a massive tentacle came smashing down on the top of the submersible, driving it completely underwater. She sailed through the air like she'd been shot from a cannon—right into Sam's arms.

He reached up and grabbed the taut line and pulled, yanking the claw free from the building so it could retract without pulling Emily any farther. Behind her, the monstrous sea beast thrashed in the Thames, sending waves as big as fishing boats crashing onto the dock.

Her shoulders hurt from being jerked like a fish on

a hook. Sam's chest was warm and broad. *I could stay here all day,* Emily thought. She glanced up into intense eyes almost as dark as his hair. "Thanks, lad."

He didn't speak. He just held her. Her heart thumped. Was he going to kiss her? Because she would like that, very much, even if she did have the faint whiff of chamber pot about her from the river.

A sound like the igniting of a gas lamp—a hiss and pop—broke through the air, destroying the moment. What the devil...?

Both Emily and Sam turned to see Griffin, the Duke of Greythorne, in wet shirt and trousers, kneeling on the deck as though he'd been struck by more than just a foul-smelling wave.

"Bloody hell," Sam whispered.

Emily followed his gaze. Her jaw dropped. *Bloody hell, indeed.*

The Kraken hovered just above the surface of the Thames, trapped in a watery bubble of bluish light. It waved its tentacles but remained held. The thing was as big as several carriages stacked together, and yet it reminded her of the glass globes her mother used to admire—the ones that were filled with water and particles of white substance that looked like snow when shook. Only this globe held the largest sea creature she had ever seen, and made it seem as ineffectual as a delicate crystal novelty.

Finley Jayne, Emily's good friend and fellow member of Griffin's little group, ran forward to help him, yanking off the helmet of her underwater suit. Finley was a pretty girl—honey-colored hair with a streak of black in the front, and amber eyes. It was no secret she and Griffin had feelings for each other, though they'd continued dancing around them since returning from America a few months ago.

"I'm worried about him," Sam said as he released Emily.

She tried to hide her disappointment. "Griffin? Me, too. He looks so tired."

Together they approached the other couple. Jasper joined them. He was a blond, green-eyed American with more charm than sense and the ability to move faster than humanly possible. Like the rest of them, he wore a diving suit. He, Sam and Finley had tried to secure cables from Emily's craft to the Kraken, so they could capture it, but the monster had proved too wily. Griffin had remained on the dock to use his own abili ties to assist.

He'd ended up capturing the bloody thing all by

himself. His power was increasing—a fact that was as frightening as it was awesome.

Finley helped Griffin to his feet. His reddish hair was a damp mess and his gray-blue eyes were heavy. "Aetheric containment field," he told them. "It will hold it until the Royal Society gets here."

His friends exchanged glances. To have conjured such a huge amount of energy from the Aether and directed it so precisely was a remarkable feat. Griffin had been honing his skills like mad as of late, though he didn't care to explain why. That had everyone worried, because previously Griffin had said he was reluctant to give too much of himself to the Aether for fear it would consume him.

Emily worried it had begun to do just that.

"Tarnation," Jasper murmured, his attention turning to the thing in the Aether bubble. "A real live Kraken. I always thought the stories were just make believe."

So had Emily, though there'd been sailors about Ireland who'd told stories of seeing the giant octopuses on their travels. Kraken were monstrous creatures that could destroy a ship and devour its crew in as little as thirty minutes. Those who had seen one up close didn't often live to tell about it, which explained why they were believed to be more myth than fact.

The Kraken they'd caught was a small one if the accounts were to be taken as truth. It was said that a mature Kraken could make a frigate look like a toy. Those large ones could overpower and snap the large ship like dry tinder.

If this was a young one, she hoped its mama didn't come looking for it. It thrashed against its prison like a child in the middle of a tantrum, but Griffin's power held fast. He refused to allow Finley to support him, and wavered slightly as he stood on the dock, pale-faced.

Emily glanced back at the Kraken and at the energy that encased it. She shivered, and not just because of her damp clothes. Griffin's power scared her at times; there seemed to be no rules or boundaries to it. The Aether was not only the spirit realm, but was made up of pure life-energy. Everything, living and dead, was part of it, fed it.

And as much as it fed Griffin, it also fed *off* him.

"You all right, Miss Emmy?" Jasper asked. While their plan had been for the underwater team to secure the Kraken, and keep it from attacking the dock, Emily had been charged with the task of trying to drive the thing to breach for capture. If that failed, the plan had been to try to force the thing out to sea once more.

"Right as rain, lad," she replied. "Though I'm a wee bit concerned about the submersible. I don't think there'll be any saving her."

The cowboy smiled. "Better to replace a ship than you, darlin'." He winked and then walked toward a group of people who had just arrived in a large vehicle pulled by several automaton horses. The back of the vehicle was a huge metal tank.

"Looks like the Royal Society has arrived," Sam announced. He hadn't even bristled when Jasper flirted with her. While this was a good sign, showing that he trusted her and was secure in their relationship, a little jealousy wouldn't have been unwelcome. She was becoming one of those foolish girls who wanted to be the center of the universe.

"That tank's not very big." She frowned. "It will fit, but just barely."

He shrugged his incredibly broad shoulders. "It should hold until they get to the aquarium. It won't be our problem regardless."

He had a point. And perhaps it was for the best if the beast had limited movement for those giant tentacles could crush a man to death with the ease of snapping a twig.

To say the society people were amazed would be an

understatement. They stared openly—not just at the Kraken but at the containment bubble, as well.

The Royal Society was scientifically driven, of course they'd be enthralled by what Griffin had conjured. Griffin didn't look the least bit concerned—another disturbing fact. He had always stressed the need for secrecy, knowing full well that society would either fear them or exploit them for what they could do.

The Society's driver backed the vehicle as close to the edge of the dock as was safe. Two men scampered up iron ladders bolted to the side of the tank to turn matching wheels. A loud clang—almost like that of a church bell too close to your head—sounded as the lid of the tank flipped open.

"How the devil do we get it into the tank?" One of the lady members asked.

A group of spectators had gathered round. Emily wasn't the least bit surprised. There seemed to be nothing Londoners liked better than a scenario in which someone might get maimed or—if the onlookers were very fortunate—killed. Unfortunately, a crowd made the chance of an accident all too great.

"Maybe I can tip the carriage over the edge of the dock," Sam suggested. "It would make driving the thing into the tank easier."

Griffin shook his head at Sam and straightened his spine. He even waved Finley off as she tried to offer him support. Emily's chest tightened. She'd known Griffin quite a while now, and she knew that stubborn expression on his face. What was he about?

The bubble containing the Kraken began to float toward the society's vehicle. The crowd gasped in unison.

"Bloody hell!" someone gasped.

Sam scowled. "Now he's just showing off."

Emily stared as the water-filled Aether field slid down into the tank as carefully and precisely as though gently placed there by a giant, invisible hand rather than the force of Griffin's will. The men on the tank slammed the top down as the bubble burst and water splashed over the side.

One of the men from the society turned to Emily and Sam, his eyes wide. "What did that?" His mustache twitched.

"It's a new scientific advancement for the navy," Emily lied, jaw clenched. "A device meant to save sinking ships or drowning men. It's still being tested."

"Brilliant," the man replied, looking slightly dazed. "Simply brilliant. Who built it? I would very much like to ask the fellow to speak at one of our gatherings."

Blast. "I cannot tell you that, sir. Only His Grace

has that information, and you know how close he likes to hold such things." And she was going to kick His Grace's backside for such a blatant display of his abilities.

The man nodded and set off toward Griffin, who looked as though he might fall down at any moment. He swiped at his nose with a handkerchief, then shoved the linen in his pocket, but not before Emily saw the blood on it.

Damn fool. He wouldn't learn his limits until his brain slid out his nostrils.

"You reckon sending him after Griff was a good idea?" Sam asked.

Emily scowled at him. "Let him tell his own lies. He wants to show off in public, that's his business. He can ruddy well figure out how to explain it." Maybe that wasn't fair of her, but she was worried about him, afraid for him, and that often manifested as annoyance in her.

Thankfully people would believe that a machine could do such things. These days folks lapped up science like it was fresh cream and they were a hungry kitten. No, machines they could forgive for doing fantastic things. People, on the other hand, were a different kettle of fish.

People like the five of them—people who weren't "normal"—scared the rest of the world. She'd read

Mary Shelley's book about the monster, Mr. Stevenson's book about Jekyll and Hyde (said to have been based on Finley's own father), Stoker's vampire novel…none of them ended well for the character who wasn't simply "human." None of them—herself and her friends—were monsters, but she didn't want to try arguing that point against a pitchfork and torch-carrying mob. To them there'd be little difference between herself and the Kraken.

Griffin's little stunt called attention to them, just as Sam would have done if he'd moved that tank with his remarkable strength. A mob would be the least of their worries if people found out about them. Better the wrong end of a pitchfork than in a cage being poked and prodded, or in a freak show. Griffin's power as a duke would help them, but she'd had to put it to the test.

The Royal Society packed up and left and the crowd dispersed, having realized that there was nothing more to see. Sam went to Griffin's side and, after a few seconds, Emily followed after him. It would be stupid for her to remain apart when the rest of the group stood together. Petty, as well.

Finley turned to her as she approached. She looked bulky in her underwater suit, but she grabbed Emily up in a fierce hug. Good thing she was already wet and chilled.

"Are you all right?"

Emily nodded. "I'll have a few bruises later, but nothing my wee beasties can't fix. You?"

Finley shrugged. "As right as I'll ever be. At least we got it." The subtle shift in her voice said more than words ever could. *We* hadn't gotten anything. Griffin was responsible for the thing's capture. If she gave herself any credit it would be that she drove it to the surface so he could seize it.

"Let's get out of here," Emily suggested. "Griffin's not looking so good."

Griffin turned to shoot her an indignant glance. "Will the lot of you stop fussing over me like I was an invalid? I'm perfectly—" His eyes rolled back in his head as he collapsed to the rough wooden planks.

"Griffin!" Finley was the first to reach him, even though Sam was closer. She gave his pale cheek a light slap. "Griff?"

"Jasper," Emily commanded, watching blood trickle from Griffin's nose at an alarming rate. "Get the carriage."

Chapter 2

"Has he said anything to you?" Finley asked Sam when they were back at King House in Mayfair. Griffin was in his room, asleep. He'd regained consciousness on the way home and insisted he was fine, he just needed to rest.

No one really believed that. But, this was his house. He was the Duke of Greythorne, and his power over the Aether had been known to topple buildings. His power had also been unpredictable as of late, so no one wanted to push him. Not because they were afraid of what he might do to them—Griffin was their friend—but because they were afraid of what he might do to himself. There was something wrong, and he wasn't sharing it with his most trusted friends.

Sam shook his head. The four of them—Finley, Sam, Emily and Jasper—were gathered in the red parlor having sandwiches and little cakes for tea. "He'll tell us if he wants us to know."

"That's the problem," Finley shot back, in no mood for his brusque tone or ever-present scowl. She was hungry and she'd tied her corset a little too tightly. "He doesn't want us to know. Which means he thinks we'll worry. Which means whatever's wrong with him is something we *should* worry about."

"Blokes are different than girls," Sam informed her— still scowling. "We don't need to talk about every little thing. You don't hear me whining when I break a nail."

Finley's own brows pulled together. "Do you ever think before you open your mouth?"

"Did I offend your delicate sensibilities?" Sam asked sweetly. He seemed to take great pleasure in riling her. "Or are you afraid Griff might say something to me he might not tell you? If he had, *I* wouldn't betray his trust by telling everyone."

Finley's shoulders straightened. She could kick him in the throat. That would remove the smug smile from his face. How did he manage to get under her skin and know what she was thinking sometimes? It wasn't like Sam was all that bright, which meant she was completely obvious in her feelings. She'd have to change that.

But she was the one who'd cradled Griffin's head on the ride home, and the one whose clothing was stained with his blood.

"No," she agreed. "You're a good little lapdog."

His humor disappeared, replaced by a scowl darker than his usual. A muscle flexed in his jaw. Finley's fingers curled into fists, her muscles tightening. If he wanted a fight she'd bloody well give him one....

"Oh, will you two please give it a rest? Just for a wee while?" Emily looked from one to the other like a school matron ready to apply a leather strap to both their backsides. "Regardless of what Griffin does or does not wish to share with us, there's no denying something is very wrong. He is not himself. As his friends it's our job to help him, not fight among ourselves over which of us knows more secrets or can better keep them."

Sam at least look chastised, though Finley imagined that had more to do with the fact that censure had come from Emily rather than a true sense of remorse.

"He's been getting worse since we returned from New York," Finley said, and the others nodded in agreement, except for Jasper, who was looking out the window at the lawn beyond.

"It started the night Mei died," the American said quietly, turning his head toward them. His handsome face wore no expression. This was the first Finley had heard him speak of that night in Manhattan when Griffin had used his abilities to prevent a group of criminals from escaping capture.

One of the criminals had his hand crushed. The other—Mei, a girl Jasper once loved—was killed. She glanced at Emily. The red-haired girl's freckles stood out on her pale cheeks, her aqua eyes wide with sorrow. Sam looked down at his teacup. The delicate china was tiny in his large hands. Finley's shoulders sagged. She was on her own, it seemed.

"You're right," she told Jasper. "It did start that night. Griffin hasn't forgiven himself for what happened. It might...be helpful if he knew you had."

Jasper nodded, his gaze drifting back to the window. It had started to rain since they'd returned to King House, where Jasper now lived with the rest of them. "I'll have a talk with him."

Silence fell around them, uncomfortable and thick. Finley took a sip of tea. It was hot and fragrant, replacing the last of the stench from the Thames that persisted in her nostrils even though she'd bathed and changed her clothes. She had put on a purple blouse and black frilly skirt that Griffin liked, but he wasn't even going to see her in it.

No one spoke. It wasn't like them to be this quiet, but it had become more and more commonplace since their return from America. They had saved Jasper from outlaw Reno Dalton, but at what price? The wretched thought refused to leave her alone.

And Griffin, who swore he trusted her, who knew so many of her secrets, wouldn't tell her what he was going through. She felt as though he was trying to push her away, even though he seemed to enjoy being with her, especially when kissing was involved.

The sound of the doorbell made her jump. She giggled giddily—foolishly—at the relief that came with it. Finally, a diversion! The others looked to be just as pleased as she was.

When the door to the parlor opened, Finley rose to her feet to greet their guest. It was the sort of behavior expected from the lady of the house, and while Griffin had never formally called her such, he hadn't told her she wasn't, either. It was just one more confusing aspect of their relationship. His aunt Cordelia was off on some sort of adventure of her own, and no one else

seemed to want the responsibility of dealing with servants and such. As someone who used to be a servant,
Finley knew how life below stairs worked.

Mrs. Dodsworth, the housekeeper, appeared in the
door frame. "Mr. Dandy to see you, miss," she said.
Only the slight tilt of her nose as she looked down it
revealed what she thought of receiving such a notorious guest.

Jack? A diversion, indeed! Outside this house, she
had very few friends, but Jack Dandy was a favorite, if
for no other reason than he always knew how to cheer
her up and often catered to her vanity. Finley grinned.
"Show him in, please."

The older woman nodded, clearly not pleased, and
left.

"Dandy?" Sam was full-on scowling now. "What
the hell does that scoundrel want?"

Finley returned his dark expression with one of her
own. "You shouldn't use words you can't spell, mutton head."

He rose to his feet, towering over her. Good grief,
had he actually *grown?* "You shouldn't invite people into
a house that is not yours."

She climbed onto the low tea table, moving the tea
service with her foot, so that they were almost nose to

nose. "This is as much my home as it is yours, man-droid." The two of them had tangled before—Finley still had nightmares about how she had almost killed him—but that didn't stop her from curling her hands into fists. *I dare you,* she thought as she glared at the dark-eyed boy. *Take a swing.*

A hand on her belly—just above the bottom edge of her corset—prevented her from getting any further into Sam's face. The opposite hand pushed against his torso. Emily stood between them, small and determined.

A rose between two thorns. The wry thought almost made her smile, but then she saw the expression on the smaller girl's face and she thought better of it.

"Get down from there," Emily commanded, her Irish brogue thickened by annoyance. "And you, Sam Morgan, sit down, you great, foolish article! Do the two of ye have absolutely no idea of how to behave as proper? You're worse than two dogs growling over the same bone."

Shame tugged at Finley's conscience, but she didn't immediately step down. She waited for Sam to move first.

"You'll be waitin' a long time if you tink she'll give in first, mate," came a familiar voice from the door.

Finley didn't have to look. She'd only ever met one

person who spoke so atrociously and eloquently at the same time. "Jack!" She jumped down from the table and ran to him, boots thudding on the carpet.

He looked the same—impeccably dressed in head-to-toe black, hair falling in waves around the points of his lapels. His complexion was as fair as his hair was dark, making him incredibly striking—a fact of which he was well aware. He picked her up as she threw her arms around him, his own closing around her, strong and warm.

"It's so good to see you!" It was true. She hadn't seen him in weeks.

He gave her a squeeze before setting her back on her feet. "A right lovely sight are you as well, Treasure. Glad to see your sojourn to the colonies done you no lasting 'arm." His dark eyes surveyed the room. "Where's 'is pompousness? I've come to speak with 'im."

Not just to see her then, Finley thought—a little glumly, were she honest. When she first met Jack she had been drawn to him, but not in the way he had wanted. Still, a girl liked attention now and then, didn't she? Especially when the bloke *she* wanted was keeping secrets.

"His Grace is indisposed," Sam informed him, stepping forward. His scowl had deepened. How was that even possible? "Next time make an appointment."

Jack was a couple of inches shorter than Sam and at least two to three stone lighter, but didn't seem the least bit intimidated. In fact, he looked amused. He tapped the end of his walking stick on the floor. "Don't get your drawers all knotted up, Goliath. If I wants to court trouble I never 'ave to leave Whitechapel. I've come into possession of some information the likes of which I believe would interest Monsieur *le duc*."

"Why don't you tell us?" Finley suggested, gesturing for him to sit. Emily had pulled Sam aside and was talking at him animatedly, pointing a finger at him and frowning. Sam looked suitably chastised. "Would you like tea?"

Jack turned the full force of his intense gaze on her. It was as though he could see right down into her soul. Instinctively, she laid a palm over her brown leather corset, as though her flesh and bone might offer some protection against the feeling that she had done something wrong.

"Mistress of the 'ouse are you, Treasure? Can't say as that I'm surprised."

Heat flooded her cheeks. Oh, good Lord, she was blushing! Blast him for embarrassing her. She raised her chin. "I'm not mistress of anything. I was just being polite."

He held her gaze—longer than was proper. It wasn't what he'd said that bothered her, but rather that he'd said it in front of the others. What she felt for Griffin was…private. Calling attention to it was very un-English of him.

And made her very aware that perhaps Jack's feelings for her were still much deeper than friendship.

"My mistake," Jack conceded, his voice soft. "Tea would be lovely, thank you."

It wasn't the first time he'd dropped that awful affectation of his in front of her. Doubtful that the others even heard him, especially Sam and Emily, who were having their own conversation, er…argument.

"Have a seat," she said, and rang the bell for a fresh pot and another cup.

Finley didn't speak to him while they waited for the tea, but her silence wasn't because she didn't know what to say—it was because Jack had gone straight to Jasper, leaving her standing by herself. Her hearing was exceptional, but she couldn't eavesdrop on Sam and Emily *and* his conversation with the cowboy.

For a moment, despite being in this beautiful house as someone who belonged there, Finley was struck by the feelings of being an outsider that had plagued her for most of her life.

She did *not* like it.

"Oi!" she cried. All eyes turned to her, but her gaze was on Jack. Perhaps she was a little mad—certainly her mind seemed to be scattered lately—but she couldn't stand to be left out, not just by Griffin, but by everyone else. "You said you had information?"

Jack arched a brow at her bad manners. It took all of her strength not to look away. "Quite," he said, moving toward the sofa. The others closed in, too, and seated themselves around the room just as fresh tea and sandwiches arrived.

Finley poured Jack a cup, fixed it how he liked it and offered it to him. She did not meet his gaze—the bounder already understood her too well.

"You certain 'is Lordship ain't available?"

"Decidedly," Emily replied, setting a strange contraption on the tea table in front of Jack. "Would you mind if I record you, Mr. Dandy?"

"Call me Jack, darling. All the pretty girls call me Jack."

Finley rolled her eyes.

Emily grinned at him, bright eyes sparkling. "No

doubt they call you many things, some of which they might even repeat in polite company."

"You come here to talk or to flirt?" Sam demanded.

Jack smiled. "Unlike you, mate, I'm able to do two fings at once." He winked at Emily before turning to Finley. "Somefin strange 'appened Thursday last—somefin I reckon you lot will find very interesting."

Finley perched on the edge of the sofa near Emily and waited for him to elaborate. Instead, Jack picked up his cup and saucer and took a sip. He didn't even slurp. Then, he reached out and took a little cucumber sandwich off the tray and proceeded to eat it with better manners than she expected.

When he moved to take another sandwich, she pushed the plate just out of his reach. "Talk first. Eat later, Jack."

His gaze narrowed, but there was a twinkle in his eye. "You've become cruel, Treasure. An 'eartless minx what delights in denyin' a man 'is proper tea. A little suspense is good for the digestion."

Was everything a joke to him? Yes, she supposed it was. To be Jack Dandy was to treat every day as a novelty and to never take anything—himself included—too seriously.

Still, he had to take some things seriously—he

wouldn't have a reputation as a lord of the criminal underworld without having done *something* to deserve it.

It was a battle of wills, one she knew she wouldn't win—not before the others decided to toss her out the window. She pushed the plate toward him. "I would hate to discombobulate your digestion."

He flashed straight white teeth and snatched another sandwich. "Fanks. So, as I were sayin', about a fortnight ago I was contacted by a bloke about circumnavigating a transportation dilemma 'e 'ad discovered."

"I thought you said it was last Thursday?" Sam demanded, stuffing a biscuit in his mouth.

Jack gave him a patently condescending look. "I'm setting the stage, chum. Creatin' a mood, if you will. Listen carefully and our pretty little ginger will explain the words you don't understand." What sort of fellow deliberately baited a creature such as Sam?

Apparently a fellow much like herself.

Sam opened his mouth to respond, but Jack cut him off. "I'm just 'aving a bit of fun. No need to get all red in the face and cosh me over the 'ead with those meat 'ooks you call 'ands. As I were saying, I was approached by a bloke who offered me enough coin to keep me mouth shut and just do the job." He plucked another sandwich from the tray.

"Which was?" Finley prodded. Honestly, he was being deliberately difficult.

Jack chewed and swallowed. He hadn't even gotten any crumbs on himself. He'd been taught proper manners, she'd bet her left arm on it. "Transportin' a crate from the docks to an underground station on the Metropolitan line."

"Which station?" Jasper asked. Finley hid her surprise that he was even paying attention. He never used to be so quiet or distant. Granted, she hadn't known him well prior to going to New York, but he had changed when Mei died, and this was not that same fellow she considered a friend.

"St. Pancras. It were a fairly large crate, weighed at least nine to ten stone. I 'ad to 'elp load it onto the carriage." He shuddered, as though the thought of manual labor was beneath him, but Finley didn't buy it.

"Where on the docks?" she asked.

"Not far from where that building collapsed a few months back." His gaze traveled to each one of them. "I reckon you're all familiar with it."

Finley's blood froze in her veins. He meant the building Griffin had brought down with his power—the building the man known as the Machinist had used as his automaton workshop. The Machinist was a man named Garibaldi, and his corpse hadn't been found when authorities searched the wreckage.

"The man who hired you, what did he look like?" Out of the corner of her eye she saw Emily's tense expression and knew her friend had the same thought she had.

"Blond and blue-eyed," Jack responded.

Emily glanced at her, sharing relief that it wasn't Garibaldi. There was no way he could have survived that building coming down on top of him. Was there?

Jack continued, "Looked almost Albinese. Great big fat 'ead. I didn't get the feeling 'e was new in town, but I weren't familiar with 'im. Bit of a Geordie, if my knowledge of dialects is up to snuff."

Finley didn't doubt he could identify a person's regional origin with three miles. "You didn't ask what the cargo was?"

He looked affronted. "Course not, but somefin about it felt off, right? I've survived on luck, intuition and not being a bloody idiot. Every instinct I 'ave told me this weren't good. So, before I delivered the crate I opened it."

He'd lost some of his swagger and the sparkle in his eyes. That couldn't be a good sign. He took a drink of tea and made a face. Perhaps he really wanted something a bit stronger. That didn't bode well. Dandy was not easily disconcerted.

"What was in the crate, Jack?"

"An automaton. I think." His accent lost much of its affectation. "Unlike any metal I've ever seen."

The unease pooling at the base of Finley's spine intensified, but it was Emily who asked, "How so?"

Jack chuckled, but there was little humor in it. "She—and it was definitely a girl—was naked, and she—" he swallowed "—she had bits of skin on her, like she was a patchwork quilt without all its pieces."

"It must have been a waxwork," Emily suggested, perhaps a bit condescendingly.

Dark eyes turned to her. "That's what I told myself—before I touched her. Skin and hair. I fancied I could see lungs beneath her metal ribs. One eye socket was empty, the other had an eyeball in it—it was the color of amber." He swallowed, and set his cup and saucer on the low table at his knees.

Finley reached out and put her hand on his arm. She'd never seen him so rattled, but then she'd only known him a few months. "It must have been a frightening sight, but it was just a machine, Jack."

He stared at her, then at the hand on his sleeve. It was as though a curtain was pulled back into place, and he was once again the Jack Dandy she knew. "No, Treasure. I don't fink it were."

She removed the hand he seemed to find so offensive. If he hadn't called her "Treasure" she'd start to wonder if he was angry with her. "Why not?"

Jack's jaw tightened. "It...*she* spoke to me."

She had asked the handsome man not to put her back in the dark, but the fleshy stub in her mouth didn't move the way she wanted and refused to form the words, so all that came out was a moaning noise.

He had looked at her in horror, as though she were a...monster. That was the word. She didn't quite know what it meant, but she knew it was right. He was disgusted by her. That made her sad, even though she wasn't sure why, except that he had looked so very pretty to her.

But then, everything looked pretty when your eyes were brand-new, as hers were. She had two now. The second one had started to appear the day after the man opened the ceiling on her wooden domicile.

Domicile. That meant home. She lifted her chin and looked around the room. The other machines had put her here after removing her from the crate. Was this to be her home now? It was ever so much nicer than the hot, smelly box, even though they had set her inside a casket of iron. At least the casket allowed her to stand upright. If only they hadn't shackled her inside, she might move about a bit. Perhaps that would ease the incessant pressure in her abdomen. It was almost unbear...

Oh.

Hot, wet liquid splashed against her feet. It was coming from inside her. Was it oil? Some sort of chemical for her inner workings? It smelled funny, but at least her belly didn't hurt. In fact, the release of the liquid felt wonderful. Whatever it was, she'd had a surplus that obviously had to be evacuated. Would this be a regular occurrence?

The door to the room she was in opened, and in scuttled two automatons. One had a shiny porcelain doll head perched atop its squat metal body, and eight reticulated limbs that made it move like an insect. The other appeared as an elderly woman in a tattered gown. It appeared as though her head had been removed at one time and reattached by a clumsy child. It was pitched forward and slightly to the side.

She tried to draw back from them, their monstrous countenances frightening, but there was nowhere for her to go while trapped in the lead box.

"I told you it was going to be female," the spider said to the woman. Its voice was like the clattering of discordant notes on a piano keyboard.

"We must find some clothing," the other replied in a voice that was almost human, but with a slight hitch. Whoever had put its head back on hadn't aligned the voice box correctly. "It would not be proper for her to be seen naked, but we can no longer keep her restrained now that biological function has begun. Bring someone to clean up her mess."

The short one made a skittering sound. It wasn't any kind of language her logic engine could identify, but she understood it, regardless. It was the language of metal, and the spider didn't like being ordered about.

A clawlike hand lashed out from the "old woman" and struck the other. "You will do as told, or face the wrath of the Master."

The Master. The mention of him made the gregorite vertebrae of her spine cold. Part of her insisted she bow to him, but another part...that strange part responsible for the gooey eyeballs in her head and the fleshy thing in her mouth, was afraid. Why would she be afraid? She was machine, and machines were not capable of feeling.

Something jumped in her chest. She looked down. Between the two swells of flesh on her chest there was a small expanse of her framework not yet covered over by skin. There, through the gleaming rungs of her chasse she spied a red, wet lump of muscle, ebbing and receding in time with the pulsing throughout her form.

What was happening to her?

The old woman came to her, every step halting, punctuated with a dry, grinding sound. Her thin lips clicked upward into a grotesque parody of a smile.

A smile with no emotion behind it. No humanity. The skin of the machine's face was gray and lax. There was something wrong with it, but what? Her mind knew she should be horrified, but not why.

And it stank. Stank like death, though she had no idea how she knew that. In fact, she didn't even know her own name. Did she have a name?

"What are you going to do with me?" she asked. The thing in her mouth was bigger now, and moved when she spoke, so that the words that came out sounded almost as they ought.

How did she know how the words were supposed to sound? Why did she know so much and so very little? Why was she so afraid?

"Don't worry, little one," the old woman said, reaching out and touching her with cold, foul fingers. "We have great plans for you."

Chapter 3

A strange young man stood up when Finley entered the dining room the next morning. He was alone at the table, a half cup of coffee and a plate with a few bites of coddled eggs and ham in front of him.

"Good morning," he said. "You must be Miss Jayne."

Finley's gaze traveled down the lanky length of him, from his reddish hair to his shiny shoes. He had a kind face, but she knew that looks could be deceiving. "And you must be?"

He offered his hand. "Silverius Isley. I'm an associate of His Grace."

She looked at his fingers. They were long and soft— the kind of hands she expected from a man wearing such a well-made jacket. Not a speck of dirt beneath his manicured fingernails. Hesitantly, she put her hand in his. "What sort of associate?"

His entire body went rigid, fingers clamping around hers like a vise. Free hand tightening into a fist, Finley pulled back but stopped when she saw his eyes. They had rolled up in his head so far only white and tiny red veins remained. His weight tugged her forward as he wavered on his feet.

Good Lord, did he belong in an asylum? Was he ill? And what was his connection to Griffin?

Her free hand grabbed his arm to keep him from falling. His body jerked once...twice...then went still. She almost dropped him as the tension drained from him and he went as limp as a rag doll in her arms.

"What...?" He looked around, noticed she was holding him. Weakly, he regained his footing. "Oh, dear."

Slowly, Finley helped him back into his chair. "You had some sort of fit."

Isley took a sip of his coffee. The hand around his cup trembled. "What I had, Miss Jayne, was a visit from an apparition."

Had she heard him correctly? And was he, as Jasper would say, "pulling her leg"? "You mean a ghost?"

He chuckled. "Your dubious tone says more than

enough, Miss Jayne. You do not believe in my particular talent."

"I don't believe in much I can't see," Finley replied
defensively.

"Yet you live in the home of a young man who regularly traffics in the world of the dead."

Fair enough. "I've seen what His Grace can do. I
don't know you."

"No, you do not. Thank you for keeping me upright.
In the past I've done myself quite a harm during a visitation." He pointed to a small scar above his eyebrow.
"I'm fortunate this is my only souvenir."

Finley eyed him warily before crossing to the sideboard to load a plate with her own breakfast. Isley was
odd, but she was starving, and her stomach didn't care
if he talked to ghosts or saw fairies. She sat down at
the table and dug into the eggs, toast and ham like a
starving beast.

Mr. Isley arched a brow but wisely remained silent.
She may not be embarrassed to eat in front of him, but
no girl liked attention called to the amount of food on
her plate, or the degree of enthusiasm with which she
dug in to it.

"The coffee is still hot," he mentioned. "May I pour
you a cup?"

She swallowed the food in her mouth before answering, "Thank you."

He tipped the silver pot over her cup and poured just the right amount of fragrant black brew, leaving room for milk and sugar.

"Good morning, all."

Finley looked up as Jasper entered the room. He was his usual tousled self. "Good morning." A glance at Isley made her pause. The young man was looking at Jasper like...well, the way Finley fantasized about Griffin looking at her. Jasper, a typical fellow, seemed completely unaware of the attention. He had no concept of just how handsome he was, which made him all the more likable in Finley's estimation.

"Jasper, this is Mr. Isley, a friend of Griffin's. Mr. Isley, this is Jasper Renn."

Jasper nodded in greeting. "Pleased to meet you."

Isley cleared his throat, a pink flush climbing his cheeks. "Likewise."

The American filled a plate and poured himself a cup of coffee. "Enjoy your breakfast," he said before leaving the room. He hadn't had breakfast at the table since moving in. He would never feel he belonged if he insisted on putting distance between himself and the rest of them.

Then again, maybe he didn't want to belong.

Isley watched him leave. "I say, is he a real American cowboy?"

Finley smiled. "He has the hat, too."

"Extraordinary." This was said with just a hint of wistfulness.

"Indeed." Isley didn't know how much. Jasper could move so fast it seemed like the rest of the world almost stopped around him. He also seemed to prefer girls to blokes, but who was she to dash Isley's apparent infatuation?

"I hope he didn't break his fast elsewhere because of me?"

Oh, poor thing. She'd gone from wariness to wanting to pat his hand. "No. Jasper often takes breakfast in one of the rooms facing the stables so he can see the horses." She didn't figure Jasper would mind her saying that. It was better than telling Isley that Jasper couldn't seem to stand the sight of any of them for long.

Mrs. Dodsworth entered the dining room. "Mr. Isley, His Grace requests that you join him in the blue parlor. If you would follow me?"

The young man dabbed at his mouth with his napkin and rose from the table. "It was lovely to meet you, Miss Jayne."

"You, as well, Mr. Isley."

He stopped in the door, and partially turned to look at her. "Miss Jayne, would you have known a young blond man with blue eyes and a small brass bar in his left eyebrow?"

Finley swallowed hard, her toast lodged in her throat. Lord Felix. He was the son of her former employer, and the last time she saw him he'd tried to force himself on her. She'd knocked him senseless. He was also dead. "I'm not sure."

He smiled slightly. "Perhaps my vision showed me the wrong person. It has been known to happen. I thought he must mean something to you."

"Why would you assume that?"

"Because the spirits showed me his murder when I touched your hand."

"I'm not letting you go alone."

Emily put down the hammer before she could be tempted to use it on Sam's metal-enhanced skull. Slowly, she turned from her workbench far below King House and faced the infuriatingly overprotective, overbearing, overly gorgeous mutton head standing a few feet away.

Not long ago in this very room she'd saved his life for

the second time when a fight with Finley turned bad. He was so very concerned with her life that he seemed to forget he was the one who had almost died. Twice.

"Are ye volunteering to come with me, then?"

"No. I'll go by myself."

She didn't try to hide her annoyance. "Oh, right, Mr. 'I'm not afraid of anything.' What happens if you encounter a chunk of metal intent on beating you into the ground?" It was unfair of her to bring it up, but he'd almost been killed by a machine once, and he'd been deeply afraid of them ever since.

So had she, and it wasn't made any easier by being able to communicate with the logic engines in the things.

"Better I face it alone than have to worry about you," he retorted.

All thought of unfairness went out the bloody window. "You foolish, ridiculous, backward—" Her tongue seized when he grabbed her by the arms and hauled her close.

"Seeing you fight that Kraken almost did me in, Em. I can't go through that again. The thought of losing you..." Sam's gaze locked with hers. "I can't live in a world without you in it."

Oh. *Oh.* A few pretty words and her heart melted.

Her resolve, however, didn't waiver. "You're going to have to accept it, boyo, because I can't wait here for you to return, wondering if I'll be able to put you back together again. You're not going without me."

"Stubborn wench."

"Thick-skulled jackanapes."

"That's your fault, isn't it? You put metal in my head, no wonder it's thick!"

She stared at him a second, fighting the laughter bubbling up inside her. It was no use; it poured out from her belly until she had to wipe her eyes, and even then it was difficult to stop.

"This is funny to you, is it?" Sam demanded.

There had been a time when he would have laughed, as well. Finley and Jasper wouldn't believe her, but Emily remembered a time when consternation and anger weren't etched into his handsome face. A time when he didn't take everything as a personal insult. A time when he hadn't treated her as though she were made of the thinnest glass.

She took his hand in his. "Smile a wee bit, Sam. Please? Just for me."

"I don't think your safety is anything to smile over." He made it sound like something nasty.

"You don't find much worth smiling over anymore."

She tried to keep the disappointment from her voice, but he stiffened at the remark, regardless.

"No, I don't." Hesitation turned his expression from anger to uncertainty. "I don't like being like this, Em. I can't seem to stop it."

Was that her fault? When she put him back together the first time, had it been a mistake? She refused to think of it like that, but there was no denying that he had changed.

She swallowed. "Do you blame me?"

He started. "No. You saved me. I wouldn't be alive if not for you."

"You wouldn't be partially metal, either. You wouldn't be so unhappy."

"Do you regret it? Do you ever wish you'd just let me die?"

Pain picrced her heart. "No, Sam. Lord, no." She reached up and took his rugged face in her hands. He was so big, so strong. So vulnerable. "I would give anything for you to be happy again."

"I'm happy when I'm with you."

Tears burned the backs of her eyes. "Oh, lad."

He picked her up as though she weighed no more than a child and set her on the workbench so that they were practically eye to eye. His size and strength should frighten her—men often did frighten her—but with Sam she never felt anything but safe. He treated her with tenderness when she was used to violence.

He was the first—and the only—male she ever thought it would be nice to have touch her.

"I have to go," she explained. "If we run into an automaton that hasn't learned language I'm the only one who can communicate with it. We'll have a device that interferes with mechanical armatures. I don't know if it will affect you or not." Meaning that this was one time when she was the best person for the job and he was not. "Finley will be with me. You know she won't let anything hurt me." Though, if metal went berserk, she was just as capable of bringing it down as Finley, perhaps more so.

"I can't tell you what to do," he said in a soft tone. "I don't want to boss you around. I just don't want you to get hurt."

She brushed a thick lock of hair back from his brow and lightly touched the furrow there. It dissolved almost immediately. There he was. There was her Sam. "Sometimes people get hurt," she told him. She'd been hurt before, but she was still alive. She was still able to feel love and physical attraction despite what had been done to her.

"But I can't put you back together," he whispered.

Mary and Joseph, but he broke her heart. "You already have, Sam." And it was true. "I can't begin to count the ways you've mended me."

He kissed her then. Her heart leaped—not in fear but in joy. Butterflies tangled their wings in her stomach. Sam's kiss and touch made her feel things she thought had been taken away from her by rough, cruel forces.

Sam cupped her face as he pulled back just enough to look her in the eye. "I don't want to lose you."

"You won't. You won't ever lose me, I promise." And she meant it. "And someday, I'm going to make it so that all you want to do is smile."

He kissed her again, and it was a long time before either one of them spoke.

Emily caught her skulking around outside the blue parlor, the horn of an ornophone against the door as she tried to listen to the conversation taking place on the other side.

Mr. Isley and Griffin were discussing ghosts, but she was having the devil of a time hearing the full extent of their conversation. Something they were doing created a low-grade noise that partially drowned out their voices. Blast it all. How was she ever to know what was going on?

"What are you doing?"

Finley jumped. Fortunately she did so quietly. She could only hope the device made it just as difficult to hear what was going on in the corridor. She tiptoed toward her friend, her finger to her lips so Emily would shush. If Griffin caught her it was going to make it that much more difficult to find out what he was keeping from her.

The library wasn't far, so Finley gestured the other girl inside and then closed the door.

"I was trying to eavesdrop on Griffin's meeting."

"That much was obvious," Emily replied disapprovingly. "Why?"

The redhead's wariness was to be expected. As good friends as the two of them had become, Emily's loyalty belonged to Griffin first. And Emily favored a more direct approach than Finley did.

"Because the bloke he's talking to says he saw Lord Felix's murder when he touched my hand." She folded her arms over her chest. "And I want to know if he is what he seems, or if he's a charlatan."

"A male medium? How interesting. Woman tends

to be the more sensitive sex when dealing with the spirit realm."

Finley shrugged. "He seemed to find Jasper quite attractive."

Emily shot her a censorious look. "That doesn't make him any less male."

Not physically obviously, but perhaps his preference gave him more of a feminine sensibility where the dead were concerned. Or maybe the whole thing was bollocks. "I don't care what he is. I just want to know if I killed the bastard!" She slapped her hand over her mouth, but it was too late; she'd said too much.

The color drained from Emily's already pale face. Just as quickly her expression went from surprise to annoyance. "Of course you didn't kill him. Scotland Yard said you were no longer a suspect. You could never kill anyone."

"Your confidence is appreciated, but you don't know that. *I* don't know that. I have no memory of that night, and it was before Griffin started helping me amalgamate my two selves." Plus, Scotland Yard thought a man had done it, but only because an "ordinary" girl wouldn't have been physically strong enough.

Finley was stronger than most men.

Small, warm hands came down upon Finley's shoulders as her friend met her gaze intently. "Do you honestly believe you are capable of murder?"

"I'd kill if I had to."

"If you didn't kill that slimy bastard when he attacked you, there's no reason to believe you could do so in cold blood. You'd never be capable of such a thing."

"That doesn't mean that someone else didn't do it for me."

Understanding dawned in Emily's eyes. "You think Dandy did it."

Finley nodded. She didn't have even the slightest doubt that Jack would kill for someone he cared about, and Lord Felix had been part of the gang of young men who followed Jack around like he was their new messiah. If he wanted to send a message about what would happen to his followers who stepped out of line, it would have been the perfect opportunity.

"I'm not afraid he did it, Em. I'm afraid he'll get caught. I don't want Jack to go the hemlock chair for me." The idea of Jack being stuck by all those needles, poisoned and left to die a slow death made her feel sick.

"Oh. Aye, I understand. But maybe he didn't do it, either. Lord Felix was an arse. I have to think he had many enemies."

"True." Finley glanced toward the closed door.

"I should have just made Isley tell me, but I was too shocked to stop him." And afraid. She had no idea what sort of man Isley might be. Had no idea if he might come back at another time to blackmail her, or use the information against her somehow.

If she had killed Felix she wasn't going to be sorry for it, but she'd hate for Griffin to think less of her. That was her true fear, and she was a foolish twit for it.

"Well, that tells you that the killer wasn't you. No one would be stupid enough to admit to a murderer that they know all about it."

"No, I reckon not." Blast Emily for being so smart and rational. It made her feel all kinds of foolish. But honestly, she'd been more afraid for Jack than for herself. Not by much, but still her worry was mostly for him.

And a little bit afraid of what it said about his feelings for her, were her fears true. You didn't kill for a casual acquaintance. Afraid because no matter how much simpler it would be to choose Jack Dandy, crime lord, over Griffin King, Duke of Greythorne, she couldn't. She chose Griffin.

Though, right now with him being all secretive and standoffish, even though everyone knew something was wrong, she sometimes wished she didn't choose him. She was good enough to be kissed but not good enough to be trusted. At least she wasn't alone there. He wouldn't confide in any of them. He might say they were all a team, but this sort of behavior made it perfectly clear that he was lord and master in this house and the rest of them just lived there.

And just who was this Silverius Isley to be given breakfast and a private audience?

"You won't hear anything," Emily told her, gesturing to the ornophone. The brass horn-shaped instrument was in need of a polish. "He uses an Aetheric amplification transducer whenever he wishes to have a completely private conversation."

"Ah, yes. Of course." What the devil was an Aetheric whatever-it-was?

"It turns Aetheric energy into sound waves," Emily explained as though reading her mind. "Basically he uses it to make just enough noise that no one can eavesdrop. I wonder who he thinks might listen at doors?"

Well, she felt fifty different kinds of ridiculous now. "I reckon I'll put this useless thing away then." She lifted the ornophone. "It made me feel like an old woman anyway."

Emily smiled—a sly quirk of her lips. "I do have a device that can dissipate Aetheric sound waves."

Of course she did, clever chit. Finley's eyes narrowed. "I thought you didn't like me eavesdropping?"

"I don't, but I don't blame you for it. And if this continues much longer I'll give you my device with my blessing. Better yet, I'll make one for all of us. Regardless of what Sam says, Griffin will not tell us if there is something wrong until it's verging on too late. Sam's so caught up in worrying about me that he can't see his best mate's in trouble."

She didn't want to think about what "too late" might include. "Had a chat with Mr. Morgan, did you?" She began walking down the corridor and Emily fell into step beside her. Intentions of eavesdropping were forgotten for the time being.

"Yes. I think we're finally beginning to understand each other. I just wish…"

"What?"

Emily looked away. "That I could make him as happy as he makes me."

"Happiness is an individual pursuit, Em. He has to let himself be happy first. You spend far too much energy worrying about him."

"I lo—I care about him." She gestured at Finley. "I may not be listening at doors, but I worry about him."

"Meow. Retract those claws of yours. I don't care if

you write sonnets about his eyes and rhapsodize about his hair. I'm just suggesting that maybe if you stopped trying to *make* him be happy he'd find happiness on his own."

"How?"

"Well, maybe he'd realize that you accept him as he is. Have you ever stopped to consider that maybe part of the reason he's unhappy is that he thinks you're unhappy with him?"

Emily stopped—obviously she hadn't considered that at all. "And perhaps Griffin keeps secrets from you for the same reason you're afraid of him discovering yours—that you'll think less of him."

Now there was a thought. "I hadn't entertained that possibility." She hadn't thought that perhaps Griffin had insecurities of his own. She was too busy second-guessing herself and worrying that he might not like her if he really knew her.

Sometimes she did reckless things just for the sheer joy of it. And sometimes she fought the urge to get into street brawls with men twice her size. Other times she felt guilty about keeping books from Griffin's library in her room because no one else could read them. It was no more fun being too good than it was being too bad. But would Griffin still want her if she was sometimes bad? He never seemed to do the wrong thing, while she sometimes deliberately set off in the wrong direction.

Although, that blatant display of his abilities at the dock had been incredibly daring.

"You want to see if cook's made any cakes?" she suggested, tired of thinking. Did blokes have any idea just how much of a bother they were? "We could make some tea and eat ourselves silly." That was the "good" option. The bad was jumping on their velocycles and driving into the east end for a little danger and excitement.

"Actually, I have another idea." Emily stopped and turned to face her. "Let's go to the St. Pancras station."

"I thought we weren't going to go until we discussed it with Griffin?"

Emily tilted her head to one side. "How long do you reckon it will be before that happens?"

She had a point there. Besides, it was something to do that would take not only her mind off Griffin, but Emily's off Sam. Lord knows they could both benefit from that!

Finley shrugged. "Why not?" She had nothing better to do. "Can we have cake first, though?" She was starving.

Her friend grinned. "Of course. One of us needs to take a por-tel with us. I told Sam I would."

Emily had created portable telegraph devices for all of them that made communication so much easier. They were also very helpful if one of them found themselves in a spot of trouble and needed help.

They stopped by the kitchen for cake and tea—Finley made a pig of herself while Emily watched with amusement. Then, they grabbed jackets and whatever supplies each needed for poking about the station. They were going to look for clues as to where the mysterious automaton-girl had been taken, and by whom. They met at the stables—where the velocycles were kept—ten minutes later.

Finley appraised Emily's various items. She looked prepared for anything. "Just what are you hoping to find there, Em?" Sometimes she wondered at the many devices and weapons her little friend made or possessed. What had happened to her that she was obsessed with making certain she and everyone around her was as safe as possible? It went beyond ordinary preparedness.

Emily swung her leg over her machine and gripped the steering bar as she kicked the stabilizing bar out of the way. "I don't know, but I promised Sam I'd be careful, so I want to be prepared for any eventuality."

That was sweet. Respectful. Finley tried to ignore a stab of jealousy as she climbed onto her own machine. Would Griffin worry about her? Would he even notice she was gone?

She wasn't certain she wanted to know the answer.

Chapter 4

She woke up with a start, a strange pounding in her chest. Was one of her parts defective? A cog off its pattern? No, it was that organic thing—that lump of muscle that pumped blood through her system.

What was blood again? Oh, yes. It was essentially the oil that kept human organisms running smoothly.

She touched her head. Inside her skull felt odd—as though her logic engine had somehow changed—had become more. Information assaulted her at an alarming rate.

She understood it. All of it.

She was learning. She was *evolving*. Her heart—that's what it was called—gave another jump.

They'd given her a name—Endeavor 312—which she didn't like, and clothes, which she did. They'd also given her access to a water closet should she need to expel fluid again. And they'd given her food and water—things that would act as fuel in her changing system. Things she would have to expel later on, only to continue taking more in. It seemed wasteful to her, but she understood the necessity.

It had been explained to her that she was the first of her kind, that she would notice changes. The spider had told her not to get emotional over them. She wasn't quite sure what emotions were, but she knew it was linked to this pounding beneath the cage that protected her internal workings.

Voices. That's what had brought her system to wake. The machines had gone to gather supplies, leaving her alone. They told her that soon others would join them. Was this them?

She rose from the horizontal rest bay. No, that wasn't what it was called. It was a bed. An odd term. *Rest bay* sounded much more accurate. Slowly, she walked across the dirt floor—it was cold against the bottom of her bare feet. She was much more aware of temperature fluctuations now, and anything else that engaged her sensory inputs. Her endoskeleton was now completely

covered by the pale membranous material that was sensitive to everything around it, including a breeze that
seemed to blow through the cavern.

It smelled of age and dirt and metal down here. She
knew she was underground because of how muted the
noise of the city was. And this was a city, because she
felt the rumble of trains, both above and below street
level.

Slowly, on limbs that felt awkward, she went to the
door of her room. It didn't want to open at first, but
one good yank solved that problem; the entire metal
and wood slab came free. She propped it against the
wall and slipped out into the main chamber.

There were boxes and crates everywhere, and more
slumbering automatons, too, though none seemed to
have the same covering that she did. They didn't wear
clothing, either. Some of them looked battle-scarred
and patched together while others gleamed with the
brightness of new metal.

Normally she would stop to inspect them all, but
she wanted to see their guests. There was another door
on the far side of the room and she moved toward it.
There was an odd-looking glass-front box mounted on
the wall—it showed the catacombs beyond the door.

She knew this because part of her was still machine and she understood.

A photographic camera had to be positioned somewhere near the ceiling out in the catacombs, not far from the door. Harnessed Aetheric energy fed the images seen through the lens of the camera to the receiver in the box with the glass front.

The visitors appeared on the glass. She grinned and hurried toward the door. Halfway there, she came to an abrupt and unanticipated stop.

Scowling, she looked down at the limbs that refused to move. She pulled and strained but to no avail. She could not move. It was then that she became aware of a humming noise and realized that she was more prisoner than guest herself.

The spot where she stood was home to a powerful magnet, one that froze the metal inside her to the spot. This was why the others felt they could leave her, leave the other slumbering machines—because there was little chance of escape.

And if there was little chance of escape, logic insisted that she was to be kept there regardless of her own thoughts on the matter.

She stared at the girls on the grainy surface of the glass, and then through a small slit in the door. There were two of them—one tall with light hair streaked with dark and another shorter one with hair that looked like ropes.

Part of her reacted to the sight of them. It was her heart again, kicking up a fuss in her chest cavity. She knew them. She didn't know how, but she had seen them before. The little one especially.

Out of the corner of her eye she saw movement and jerked her head around. For a moment she was terrified of the strange girl staring at her from just a few feet away. The girl had curly red hair, honey-colored eyes and pale skin. She was tall and slender and dressed in ill-fitting clothes.

The girl was her. It was nothing but her own reflection staring back at her from the scuffed surface of a long, framed mirror. She reached up—it took real effort to lift her arm under the magnet's pull—and touched her hair, then looked back at the girls outside. They walked past the door to where she was as though they didn't even see it.

But she saw them. Or rather, she saw *her;* the red-haired girl. Her mother.

Somehow, in what was left of her logic engine memory capacitors, she recognized a physical connection between herself and that tiny girl. She recognized another connection with the taller girl, as well, but not as strong. She reached forward, but the two couldn't see her. She opened her jaw to cry out, but only a low keening noise filled the room. The fleshy thing in her mouth still didn't work properly.

To her left yet another door opened. The old woman stood there, and she did not look amused. Her disapproval was made disconcerting given the odd angle of her head. She looked like a corpse that had been reanimated after its neck was broken, though how she knew that was an apt description was a mystery.

"What are you doing?" the woman demanded. The hitch in her voice box sounded worse. "Were you trying to leave?"

"I heard voices," she confessed, pointing at the glass, but her gaze was pulled past the old woman, into the room behind her. It was a sterile place, filled with soft lights and scads of machinery.

The badly repaired automaton pulled a switch on the wall, and the magnetic force abruptly disappeared. Meanwhile, her companion skittered toward the door, blocking her view of the catacombs. It didn't matter—the girls had passed by and were almost out of sight.

What interested her now was inside that forgotten room. She walked toward it and peeked over the thresh-

old. Tubes and wires ran from a framework of machinery bolted onto the ceiling to a long metal containment
tube with a thick glass cover. Inside the tank she could
see the form of a man suspended in a green, viscous
fluid. A mask covered his nose and mouth, and a hose
ran from the mask to the inner wall. A bellows outside
the tank rose and fell in a steady rhythm that matched
the rise and fall of the man's chest.

Apparatuses hummed and buzzed, clicked and
chirped. Bladders filled with liquids hung from hooks,
their tubes attached to one larger hub on the outside
of the tank. One thicker tube ran inside and was em-
bedded in the man's forearm. Were they giving him
medicine? Sustenance? Poison?

No, they weren't trying to kill him. They were trying to save him. As soon as she realized it, she knew
who he was.

"Get away from there!" the old woman snapped,
shoving her out of the room. Her voice hummed with
an odd metallic echo. She smelled bad, and her gown
gaped where it was missing a button, showing a stained
chemise beneath the dirty silk. She shut the door.

"You've no business in there. None whatsoever. You
were made for one purpose, to learn and understand. To
be the perfect vessel. You should be content with that.

It is a great honor that awaits you, little one. If you fail, you will doom us all. You will doom him. Now, back to your room. There are books there for you to read."

Reading. That was the deciphering of words upon a page so that they told a story. Yes, it was one of her favorite pastimes, though she was certain she'd never done it before. In fact, she knew she hadn't done it before, because she had no idea how to figure out what the letters meant when they were bunched together.

As she glanced over her shoulder at the door of the man's room, she was also certain of something else: if the red-haired girl was her mother, then the man being kept alive in the glass-and-metal tube was her master.

"Well, this was a rather dismal waste of time," Finley commented as she and Emily worked their way through the dank darkness of the catacombs toward an exit. While their excursion had yielded a Roman coin, a few skeletons and a host of belligerent rats, it had not produced any information to support Jack's story.

She hadn't even found anything to hit. Kicking rubbish and old bottles didn't afford the same satisfaction.

"Do you think Dandy lied to us?" Emily asked.

Finley shook her head and wrinkled her nose as a whiff of something that smelled suspiciously like sewer assaulted her. "Jack manipulates with charm and power. He doesn't lie so much as wrap the truth in temptation."

"You've given it considerable thought, haven't you?"

Despite Emily's teasing tone, Finley stiffened and made a point of shining the small but powerful lamp Emily had given her on the catacomb wall. "He's my friend."

"Oh, now don't go getting all bent out of shape. I'm just teasing, lass."

"I'm sorry, Em. I reckon I'm more thinly skinned than I thought."

"No need to apologize. I ought to have known better than to poke you when Griffin's being such a dunderhead."

"Dunderhead," Finley scoffed, unable to keep from smiling. "I can think of a few stronger names to call him."

"No doubt they'd be more succinct." Her friend grinned but quickly turned serious once more as she shone the beam of her light around them. "Other than some tracks in the dirt I haven't seen anything out of sorts. You?"

Finley shook her head. "If the automaton is down here they've done a bang-up job of hiding it, and any tracks it might have made."

Emily glanced over her shoulder. "I feel like someone is watching us. Did you hear that?"

"It sounded like a moan." Finley aimed her light in the direction of the sound. "I don't see anything."

"It could have come from anywhere. This place is bad for echoes."

"And plenty of things that could have made such a sound."

"Don't remind me. I've heard that there are people who live down here, and strange creatures unlike anything you'd see street-side."

Finley scratched her back. "Now you've got me thinking we're being watched, too." She'd rather take on a stronger opponent she could see than tangle with a weak one she couldn't.

"Paranoia's contagious. I don't see a ruddy thing and I'm hungry. Let's go back to the house. I think I have spiders in my hair."

Just the thought made Finley shudder. Blood didn't bother her, nor did violence, but the thought of something crawling on her…well, that was enough to make a girl scream and run about like an idiot. There was just something sinister about something with so many legs, especially if they possessed wings. It wasn't natural.

"Might as well," she agreed. "I don't think we're going to find anything."

"Poor thing. I wonder if she's being looked after."

It took a moment longer than it should have for her to figure out what Emily was talking about. "The automaton?"

"Aye."

"It's a machine, Em. I'm fairly certain it can look after itself." Not to mention it could break both the arms of a full-grown man without trying very hard.

"It's not just a machine." Emily looked outraged that Finley would even think such a thing. "If it was indeed covered in bits of flesh, then it has been exposed to organites. Either she's badly injured and decomposing, or her skin is not yet fully formed. Regardless, she most certainly cannot look after herself."

"You think she's like the Victoria automaton?" The thought of that awful thing put a bad taste in her mouth. It had looked so much like the queen that she'd spent several days thinking someone was going to arrest her for ripping its head off. The thing had been so human-like that destroying it felt like murder.

"We both know what the beasties are capable of doing. They helped repair Sam's heart, treated injuries. They're the reason we're...evolved. I have no doubt that she's very much like the mechanical majesty. By the time the organite process is completed, I reckon she'll be a living, breathing girl with a gregorite skeleton and a great capacity for learning. I've no idea what someone might want with her. There are so many possibilities."

"I wouldn't recommend thinking on it too hard," Finley suggested with a grimace. "I've heard stories about what some men like to do to automatons. Some women, too."

Emily held up a hand. In the dark her shirt was so very bright it made her look a little tanned, though she often burned more than anything else. "I don't want to know, thank you very much."

Finley cast a sideways glance in her direction, her expression dubious. "Whenever anyone says that it's because they already know or have a fairly good idea."

"I know lots of things, but that doesn't change the matter of me not wanting to speak of them. I'm not the fragile little doll everyone seems to think I am."

She snorted. "Nothing fragile about you, you mad Irish harpy." Finley waited until she had gotten a smile in return before pressing on. Now was as good a time as any…. "Em, did somebody hurt you?"

Emily came to an abrupt stop. Her eyes were wide, but her jaw was firm, as though something inside her was trying to force its way out and she was determined to control it. "I don't know what you mean," she said finally. When her expression went completely blank— even her eyes—Finley knew she'd struck a nerve, knew she was right. She wished she wasn't.

"If you don't want to talk about it, that's fine. I don't want to pry, but if you do…I'd like to listen." She began walking again to let her friend know she wasn't going to pressure her.

"How did you know?" Emily asked a few moments later when the silence between them had stretched on.

Finley shrugged. Good Lord, where was the bloody exit? "For a while I've suspected something had happened." Suspected and wished her friend would share with her, so she could share, as well. Lord Felix hadn't been the first bloke to try to force himself on her, but he'd been the most frightening, and not just because he would have hurt her badly, but because of how badly she had wanted to hurt him for trying it.

"I should have known you'd figure it out. Of course you would."

Was that a compliment or a judgment? Maybe neither. No one who had ever been hurt in such a manner would treat someone else's experience as a positive thing, and they certainly wouldn't cast blame.

"Do you want to talk about it?" This was what girls who were friends did, right? Talked about things that had happened to them, traded secrets. Emily was only the second friend she'd had since her twelfth birthday, and the first one had been her employer so it didn't really count. She had no idea how to handle this sort of situation.

Only she knew that she would like five minutes alone with whoever had hurt Em. Five minutes and a cricket bat.

"Not really." Emily looked straight ahead. "Not now. It was a boy I'd known most of my life. What's important is that he might have gotten my body, but he couldn't touch my heart or my soul." She turned her head toward Finley, gaze bright. "I've never told anyone else this, but I had my revenge on him later."

Finley prided herself on having a decent imagination, but she couldn't begin to fathom the sort of suffering a girl as intelligent and determined as Emily could exact from such a bastard. She thought about the boot print she herself had left on Lord Felix's forehead, and how good it had felt. "Did that make it easier?"

"It did, a little. I felt like I got a piece of myself back. Please don't say anything to the boys. Sam doesn't know. I'm not sure I ever want him to."

"And he won't ever—not from me. But doesn't he frighten you a little?" He intimidated her at times, and she had almost killed him. He was so big, so strong. So angry. Even though she'd caught glimpses of lightness in him over these past few months, he normally stomped about as if a thundercloud hung over his head.

Emily smiled. "Nah. Sam makes me feel safe. Sometimes too safe. I think that's why I fight him so often. I refuse to hide behind him. I don't want him to stand in front of me and shield me. I want him to stand beside me. With me."

Finley understood, so she nodded. What could she possibly say?

Small, warm fingers tangled with hers and squeezed. Emily had taken her hand and was smiling at her in a way that made her chest tight. "Thank you for caring enough to ask, but also not to push. I'd forgotten what it was to have a best friend before you came along."

Oh, blast. Finley's throat felt as though it was closing up on itself, and her eyes burned most uncomfortably. She didn't trust herself to speak, so she pulled her hand free and wrapped her arms around the Irish girl, lifting her off the ground in a fierce hug that made her squeal with laughter.

They walked the remainder of the distance to the

exit in comfortable silence. It wasn't until they were almost out that Finley realized she no longer felt as if they were being watched. They hadn't encountered anyone else in the catacombs, hadn't even seen a sign of humanity in that area.

So who could have been watching? And why?

Something dropped to the ground beside her. She whirled around, ready to fight. Emily pulled an Aether pistol from the holster on her belt.

It was a rat. There was another one on a ledge above their heads—no doubt the first one's mate. The one above them had a button in its teeth that looked to be mother-of-pearl.

She and Emily exchanged sheepish glances. "I reckon we were being watched after all," she joked.

Emily shook her head, putting her pistol away. "Let's go home. There's nothing down here."

Finley agreed, and when they rounded the next corner they saw light from the exit ahead. It was odd for Jack to have been so wrong, but whoever had the crate must have moved it that same day. There was nothing down here to be worried about, except a rat with a button in its mouth.

Nothing at all.

Chapter 5

If it were possible for people to be the weather, then Sam Morgan would be a thundercloud—dark, tumultuous, as gorgeous as he was intimidating. He watched the girls approach from his bedroom window.

"He looks like he is on the verge of imploding," Finley commented. They were walking back from the stables where they'd left their velocycles.

Emily smiled, glancing up. Her gaze met Sam's for a second before he dropped the curtain. "That he does." But she considered it a victory that he hadn't tried to follow her, that he had trusted her to go with Finley and to return in one piece.

"Gadzooks. You like it when he's all scowly and thumping his chest."

Sometimes, thought Emily, Finley was infuriatingly intuitive. Although, perhaps she underestimated her friend's intelligence. Perhaps she didn't hide her feelings as brilliantly as she thought.

"It lets me know he cares," she admitted. "It's not as though he's the type to say what he's feeling." Today was turning out to be a champion for sharing secrets. Why not tell Finley the shocking thoughts she sometimes had about Sam? Intimate thoughts based on pictures she'd seen in a book in Griffin's library…thoughts of her and Sam doing some of those things—things she thought she'd never want to do with anyone. "What?"

Finley stared at her as they crossed the garden terrace to the French doors. "Your face is burning so bright, I'm afraid for the draperies. Are you all right?"

Fortunately, no one ever died of embarrassment. "Must be the sun. I always end up looking like a tomato."

"Right," her friend drawled. "Because the sun is so very hot through those thick rain clouds."

"Oh, shut up!" Emily laughed despite herself. "I'm blushing and I've no intention of explaining why."

A slow grin spread across the other girl's pretty face.

Eyes the color of honey twinkled as she opened the ter-race door. "Oh, is that the way of it, then?"

Emily swept past her into the house. "'Tis." Her mirth faded when she saw Sam waiting for her. He looked relieved to see her. That was almost as good as happy. He'd been worried, that was obvious. She could assume he thought she couldn't take care of herself, but she knew that wasn't it. Sam just thought he could look after her better than anyone else.

It was sweet when she thought about it. Somewhat.

Even Finley noticed the difference in his expression, though he wore his usual frown. She took one look at him and turned to Emily. "Right. I'm going to go… do that…thing I have to do."

"Griffin wants to see you," Sam said in a tone that made Griffin sound like the matron at a strict school.

"Does he?" Finley's jaw set stubbornly. "I don't know if I have time. I'm going to be terribly busy."

"Doing that *thing* you have to do?" he inquired. Was he actually teasing Finley? He used to make sport of his friends quite often before his accident.

"Quite." Finley lifted her chin. "It's very important."

For a moment, Emily thought Sam might actually smile. He shrugged. "I don't care what games the two of you play with each other. You're both mad as far as I'm concerned."

As Finley walked past him, she gave him a sweet smile. "Maybe you can find out why she's the color of a ripe tomato."

Emily's cheeks heated once more, and she bit the inside of her mouth to keep from laughing. She couldn't laugh, not when Sam might think it was directed at him.

Finley had barely closed the door before he turned to her. "Did you find anything?" His eyes narrowed. "You are the color of a ripe tomato. Are you all right?"

The concern in his voice was as sweet as it was sometimes annoying. She had to remind herself that he didn't think she was fragile, he was just afraid. Sometimes she wondered if he realized just how afraid of the world he really was.

She shook her head. "Not a ruddy thing, unless you count a couple of wee rats."

"Did one bite you?" He started toward her. "Let me look."

She held up her hand, palm out to keep him from smothering her with concern. "Sam."

He stopped, arms folding over his chest, pulling his white shirt tight across his broad shoulders. He looked like he should be a circus strong man. She could literally climb him like a tree and have no more effect than a kitten.

"What?"

"I'm fine. Not a scratch. You're being irrational."

To her surprise his posture relaxed, and he dragged a hand through his hair. "I'm sorry, Em. I know it's mental, but I can't seem to help it. When we're apart I feel…wrong."

Her throat tightened. Had he any idea what he'd just admitted? No, she'd wager he hadn't.

"I just want you to be safe," he added.

Did he somehow know that she'd been hurt before? Because he sounded like her father, who had wanted to keep her in the house where no one could touch her. He hadn't wanted to let her do anything or go anywhere. What neither he nor Sam seemed to realize was that safety couldn't be controlled. The boy who had hurt her was a friend of one of her brothers, a boy who often walked her home from school so she'd be "safe." She had trusted him as much as her brothers, and he'd repaid her by violating that trust in the worst possible way.

And then, once she healed, she made certain he would never hurt anyone again.

In the end, her father's fear was what had made her accept Griffin's offer of employment, because if she'd stayed she would have let her father keep her locked up and let that fear overtake her.

She didn't want fear to consume Sam. She didn't want it to drive a wedge between them.

She took his big hands in each of hers, lifting them to kiss his slightly scarred knuckles. When she lifted her gaze to his, she caught him looking at her as though she'd hung the stars and the moon.

That look gave her strength. "I love you, Samuel Morgan. I love that you want to protect me, but you have to trust me to do that for myself. You have to let go of this fear of what might happen, because it will drive you mad. If you can't do these things then there's no future for us. Do you understand what I'm saying to you, lad?"

Sam nodded, looking for all the world like he'd just been hit in the face with a shovel. "You love me?"

Of course, that would be the part he grabbed on to. The boy's head was thicker than rock. "Aye. You're stubborn and scowly and you drive me to distraction, but you're the finest thing I've ever laid eyes on. I love you right down to the soles of my feet."

His arms closed around her. "Emmy, I—" He was interrupted by the door opening. It was Jasper.

"Beg pardon," the cowboy said, looking back and forth between them. "Am I interruptin'?"

"Yes," Sam growled. "Get out."

"Sorry, friend, but I need your muscles." Jasper didn't look all that sorry. "Got a stable hand pinned beneath some crates Griffin had delivered. We can't move 'em, not without the risk of injuring him further."

Sam sighed—Emily could feel it beneath her hands as well as hear it. "I'll be right there." He looked down at her. "Can we continue this conversation when I get back?"

She nodded, feeling disappointed yet giddy. The way he looked at her...well, she knew the next time they were alone was going to be very *interesting*.

"I have some work in the greenhouse. Come find me when you're done."

He smiled—actually smiled! "I will." Then he kissed her on the forehead and followed after Jasper.

Emily grinned, even giggled a little. It was foolish but she didn't care. She couldn't contain it any longer.

She was still smiling when she entered the greenhouse a little while later. Her cat—a sleek and gleaming automaton the size of a panther—was already there.

She'd sent a command for it to join her before leaving the house. It made her feel safe, could assist in some experiments and was company for her. It was sitting by the wall, very quiet and still. She'd leave it there until she had need for it.

The greenhouse was one of her babies, and it was the most modern of botanical gardens inside, complete with an underground grotto built to mimic the one beneath Griffin's country house where the organites had been discovered. Here, she bred a small colony of the wondrous creatures not only for their use, but to study, as well.

She'd barely gotten her gloves on when the door opened. "Done already?" she asked with a grin, expecting to see Sam when she turned.

But it wasn't Sam standing there. It was something she thought she'd never see again. "You." She whirled around to look for a weapon, but something struck hard against her head. Stars danced before her eyes as she fell to the floor.

Sam, she thought. And then there was nothing.

Griffin King was thought to be one of the handsomest young men in the Empire. Adding to his attractiveness was the vastness of his fortune and the fact that he was a duke. Yes, many a young lady would fling themselves in front of a carriage for a chance of winning his favor.

If they could only see him now, Finley thought, more than a little peevishly. His reddish-brown hair was a riot of untamed curls and he hadn't shaved for several days. The skin under his eyes was bruised-looking and the smell of laudanum clung to him like cologne. Since he was hardly an addict frequenting opium dens, she suspected he'd been taking the bitter, vile stuff to help him sleep.

It obviously wasn't working, because he looked as though he hadn't slept properly in days. Weeks, perhaps. He had lost weight since returning from New York, and spent more time by himself but, more important, he spent less time with her. They had admitted having feelings for each other in America. They had kissed. Several times.

They had kissed since, as well. At first they spent time together, but now...now Griffin rarely wanted to be alone with her, and when he was it had become painfully obvious that his mind was somewhere else.

Just smashing for a girl's confidence, that was. Nothing like having a bloke's attention wander when you were doing your best to divert him.

Finley had had about enough of this nonsense. There was something wrong with him and she was going to find out what it was if she had to hang him by his ankles over London Bridge until he gave in and confessed. Seeing him waste away like this…seeing him obviously suffer and not being able to help him was too painful to continue.

She went to his room as Sam had instructed, and knocked on the door. When he wouldn't open it, she climbed out the window of her own room, eased along the narrow ledge to the first of his windows and let herself in without being invited.

He was at his desk where he had apparently fallen asleep. He appeared neither surprised nor happy to see her despite having requested her presence. In fact, he looked as though her company was the last thing he wanted, though at least he didn't seem angry.

If he didn't want to kiss her anymore, he should be a man and say it to her face rather than treat her like some sort of doxy. She would rather be stranded on a deserted island with Sam than have Griffin reject her, but she couldn't stand it any longer.

"What the devil has afflicted you?" she demanded, cringing at the sharpness of her tone. She sounded just like that harpy of an aunt of his. She'd tried to be patient with him, but enough was enough. There was something *wrong* with him, and it scared her to death.

She hated being scared.

"I'm fine," he replied, rather dismissively. "Just a little under the weather. You should go so you don't come down with it also."

Finley folded her arms over her chest. "Sam told me you wanted to see me."

Griffin's brows lowered over his gray-blue eyes. "No, I don't."

That cut. "You don't have to be an arse about it." Blast, she was going to cry. She'd never cried over any other bloke but him, and part of her hated him for it.

He looked defeated. Frustrated. Sorry. "Fin, that's not what I meant." Slowly, he rose to his feet. He walked as though each step took every ounce of energy he had. When he reached her, he put his arms around her.

He needed to bathe, and the rough stubble on his chin scratched her temple, but Finley didn't care. She wrapped her arms around his waist and tried to ignore the fact that she could feel his ribs.

"Let me help you," she murmured.

"You can't, love. No one can."

She didn't believe that. She refused to believe it. "Tell me what's wrong."

He kissed her hair. "I wouldn't know where to begin."

She lifted her chin to gaze up at him. His eyes were glassy, and their embrace was less of a hug and more of her holding him upright. That was *it*. This had gone on long enough. If he wanted to keep secrets, he was entitled to have a few, God knows she did, but she wasn't going to stand around and watch him fade.

"Are you dying?" she asked.

He looked surprised. "I don't think so." And then a shrug. "I don't intend to."

She didn't like the sound of that, but if he wasn't dying at this moment then they could still fight whatever it was that had a grip on him.

And if there was one thing Finley knew how to do, it was fight.

"Sit," she commanded. He dropped onto the deacon's bench beneath the window she had crawled through. She closed the curtains just in case there was a draft. Then, she went to the small wooden box on his desk and pressed the button for the kitchen. A few seconds later a voice crackled from the horn. "Yes, Your Grace?"

"Mrs. Dodsworth, this is Finley. His Grace is in need of food and lots of it. Some tea and scones, as well, please."

"Right away, Miss Finley." She thought she could hear the older woman smile.

With that done she then went into Griffin's private bath. His room was decorated in shades of chocolate and cream, but his bath was much more colorful. The walls were rich cinnamon, the drapes a dark purple. Golds and reds added to the exotic feel. The tub was huge, claw-footed and equipped with a hose for a standing bath, as well. The outside of the tub was painted with colorfully adorned elephants, which he had once told her were inspired by a trip to India.

She'd seen pictures of India in a book once.

Finley turned the taps and dipped her fingers under the faucet until she was certain the temperature was right. She put the stopper over the drain and added a tiny bit of scented oil to the rising water.

She went back into the bedroom. Griffin was where she'd left him, his head against the wall. Had he fallen asleep?

The food would take a bit, so she crossed the carpet to where he sat, bent down and tucked him over her shoulder. Then, she stood.

"Fin?" he asked sleepily. "What are you doing?"

"What you haven't," she replied. He wasn't the only one who could be cryptic. She carried him into the bathroom, where she set him on his feet once again and removed his dressing gown. Then, her fingers went to the buttons on his shirt.

He stared at her hands. "Are you undressing me?"

"I most certainly am."

"I can do that."

"Obviously you can't—because you haven't and you stink."

"Sorry," he mumbled. Was he drunk? No, she didn't smell whiskey on him. There was a slightly sweet smell...laudanum? Didn't he use that to sometimes enhance his abilities? Had he become dependent upon it? That would explain so much.

"Lift your arms," she commanded, and he did. She pulled his shirt over his head and tossed it on the floor.

Griffin was nowhere near as big as Sam, and that was fine by her. He had broad shoulders and a narrow waist. The muscles in his arms and stomach were all the more pronounced with his recent weight loss, and his ribs were like blades beneath his skin. Still, the sight of him was enough to take her breath. She wanted to trace her fingers over the veins beneath his flesh just to see where she'd end up.

She hesitated—only a moment—before moving on to his trousers. What was that saying? He who hesitates is lost? She undid the buttons. His fingers closed around hers.

"Finley."

She met his gaze and held it.

He didn't tell her to stop. She'd started this, and if she didn't finish it, he wouldn't.

She pulled his trousers down—all the way to his feet. He wasn't wearing socks, so once he stepped out of the trousers that was it. He was naked.

Finley quickly stood up, before curiosity got the best of her. Griffin watched her, a strange expression on his face. An expression that made her tingle all over.

"Into the tub," she instructed.

He did as he was told. She could see his vertebrae as he lowered himself into the water. He wasn't quite skin and bones, but he'd get there soon enough.

He sighed.

Finley rolled up her sleeves and turned off the water when the tub was almost full. Then, she grabbed his soap and a washcloth and set to work. She washed his chest and his underarms, then his back. There was something terribly intimate about this moment that went beyond the fact that she wanted to crawl into the tub with him and see what happened next. She felt closer to him than she had in weeks.

There was a knock on the bedroom door, and she went to answer it. It was Mrs. Dodsworth with the food. The housekeeper took one look at her and asked, "Do you require assistance, Miss Finley?"

"No, thank you, Mrs. D. I've everything under control."

The older woman smiled. "You're a good girl, my dear. Just what His Grace needs—someone to take him in hand."

Finley didn't think that meant quite what came to mind.

When the housekeeper left, Finley returned to the bath, where Griffin reclined in the tub. A fine layer of suds floated on top of the water, keeping her from peeking and turning this moment into something she hadn't intended. There'd be time for that later. Right now, she needed to wash his hair.

She poured bathwater over his head, then lathered his hair with the same soap she had used to wash the rest of him. She used fresh water from the hose to rinse it away.

There was one thing left to do. She lathered a brush with shaving soap and applied it all over the stubble on his face. He eyed her cagily, looking more alert. "Have you done this before?" he asked, wiping soap from his lips and making a face when some got in his mouth.

"Of course." Once. She'd shaved her stepfather when he had an injured hand. He never let her do it again. She placed the edge of the blade against his neck and stroked upward. Perfect. He moved his head to give her better access, and made faces that made it easier for her to shave his face. When she was done, she rinsed the soap away and handed him a towel.

She left the room as he began to stand. "I'll get you a fresh dressing gown." She wasn't certain but she thought he might have chuckled.

Finley found a dark wine velvet dressing gown in his armoire and snatched it from the hanger. When she turned to take it to the bath, she jumped.

Griffin stood before her, warm and damp, with a towel wrapped around his lean waist.

She looked down. Even his feet were perfect. Then, she let her gaze drift lazily upward, lingering on his stomach and chest. A girl could only resist so long before curiosity won.

"Thank you," he said. His voice sounded rough. She liked it.

"You're welcome. You should eat."

"I will." He took a step toward her.

Her heart began to pound. Her mouth went dry.

Another step. He was so close she could feel the

warmth of his skin. He reached out and wrapped his fingers around the back of her neck as he closed the distance between them.

When his lips touched hers Finley dropped the dressing gown. He kissed her like he thought he might never get another chance, setting her heart pounding at a terrible pace. His other arm went around her waist, pulling her against him.

Her hands slid up his arms, curving over his hard biceps, over his shoulders and up his neck to tangle in the damp curls of his hair. If he stopped anytime soon she'd break both his arms. Her heart slammed against her ribs while other parts of her tingled and came alive with trembling excitement. Griffin was the first bloke—the only—that had ever made her contemplate doing something rash, scandalous.

They were alone in his room. This was his house. His aunt Cordelia wasn't around and nobody cared what they did. When he touched her she wanted...

If he drew her to his bed she wouldn't stop him. What did that say about her? Everything she'd ever been taught as a girl insisted that such a feeling was wrong— that only "bad" girls had those sort of thoughts.

But her heart didn't care. *She* didn't care. She wasn't like other girls, would never be like other girls.

He tore his mouth away from hers, even as she tried to pull him back. "Finley, I—"

She pushed against him and kissed him again. He wasn't stronger than her, would never be stronger than her, not physically. The lights in his room flickered, reacting to a spike in his Aetheric energy. The Victrola in the corner began to play a recording of Beethoven's *Moonlight Sonata,* music that sent a shiver down her spine.

They were moving. She held his head so he couldn't even think of ceasing to kiss her, and now they were indeed moving across the floor toward his bed. Wait... her feet weren't moving. How could she move without out her feet?

There was no floor beneath her feet. They were *floating.* Griffin's power wrapped around them like a blanket or a warm breeze, and carried them toward the bed. Finley's heart quickened. This was it. She refused to think about what could be so wrong with him that he tossed his morals aside, and kissed him as though she might never get a chance to again.

Her legs nudged the side of the bed. Her stomach fluttered.

The door flew open with a loud crash. Finley landed in a graceless heap on the bed—better than the floor—

and looked up to see Griffin glaring at Sam. She glared at the behemoth, as well.

Sam didn't apologize. Didn't even blush. He took one look at the two of them and didn't even seem to care that he'd interrupted something important. In fact, he looked terrified.

"It's Emily," he said. "She's been taken."

Chapter 6

Emily woke with a pounding headache.

Groggily, she put her palms flat on the floor and pushed herself into a sitting position. Her stomach rolled threateningly.

What was she doing on the floor? And why did it smell like old dirt and machinery?

She didn't want to open her eyes. It was going to hurt when the light hit them, she just knew it. But she also knew that the stickiness on her face and temple was probably blood, and that she was probably in trouble.

She opened her eyes.

Trouble was right. She was in some sort of cell with a cool, dirt floor and rough stone walls. The door was heavy iron with little more than a square in it for looking in or out. There were no windows, just one dim light—which was the only good thing about this situation. There was a small cot made up in homey quilts that looked surprisingly cozy, and a chamber pot in the far corner.

Yet she'd been dumped on the floor like an old rug.

And there were books. Stacks of books, and bits of machinery, as though her captors wanted to keep her entertained. There was also a row of pegs on the wall closest to her, and on those pegs hung several changes of clothing—her own clothing. That wasn't good. Clothing meant they had taken her intentionally, and that they intended to keep her for a while.

Slowly, she pushed herself to her bare feet, bracing her hand against the rough wall to keep from falling as her head threatened to explode. What the devil had they coshed her with? An iron bar?

No. She'd been struck by an arm. A metal arm. Automatons had abducted her from King House. Why? Who had sent them? And why would they take her? Yes, she was the smallest and the weakest of their makeshift family, but it wasn't as though she was anyone important.

Unless, of course, the people behind her abduction

knew about her "talent" with machines. That was impossible, of course. However, her knowledge of mechanics, logic engines and invention wasn't something she ever sought to hide. She'd even had some of her papers on the topic of the future of automation and the possibility of "adaptable" machines published by the Royal Society.

But machines didn't need sophisticated logic engines to learn and adapt. She knew this because of the Queen Victoria automaton the Machinist had constructed.

Queen Victoria. The memory flooded her mind, bringing a rush of dizziness that made her want to vomit. She had seen that awful creature before being knocked out.

Once it had looked like a real person, moved and acted like a real person, but all of its organic compounds had been taken from the actual queen. A flesh-and-metal hybrid that could adapt and change because the organites in its living tissue made it sentient.

She thought they had destroyed it. Obviously someone had put it back together and hadn't done a very good job of it. If it was running about on its own, this was very bad, indeed. The Machinist had programmed it to take the place of the true queen. Was it still trying to obtain that goal? Or had it moved on to something else?

The machine that had ripped Sam apart had acted against its programming because of organite infestation. Someday another automaton would do the same thing and then the organites wouldn't be their secret—not anymore. And if it wasn't machines, it would be someone looking into all the "special" humans that seemed to be cropping up. Eventually people were going to want the beasties for themselves, and then the world would be in a lot of trouble.

But that was not what she needed to fret over at this time. She'd never been the sort to fly into histrionics and she wasn't about to start now. She had survived worse things than being kidnapped, and she would make it through this, too. She would survive. She would escape, and she would put an end to the "Victoria" once and for all.

First item of business was to clean up the blood and give herself a thorough inspection. Fortunately, there was also a looking glass in the room. It was ancient, its wooden frame warped and scarred. The mirror itself wasn't in much better shape, but it didn't matter that it made her appear as long and as wiggly as an apple peel, she just needed to see the damage.

The wound on her head looked worse than it was, as those injuries often did. Once she cleaned up the blood she could see that it was more of a lump than a cut. A nasty bruise was beginning to form around the area, and she realized she was most likely concussed. Fortunately for her, she had enough organites in her system that she'd heal much quicker than she ought.

After cleaning up and inspecting herself for bruising, wounds or perhaps injection sites, she began poking around her surroundings, learning every inch of the cell. As she examined the door for a possible weakness, the heavy iron slab swung open. She jumped back to keep from being struck. The lump on her head throbbed in punishment, and her stomach clenched as the room seemed to swim around her. Blasted concussion.

Moving quickly was not good. She lurched back and stumbled as the back of her legs met the cot. She sat down hard. That hurt her head, too, but at least she wasn't in danger of falling down—or was closer to the floor if she did.

Long, multiple-jointed legs entered the room first. The creature that crossed the threshold resembled a large metal spider, with a baby doll head perched on top. Its logic engine whirled and clicked, but Emily had the feeling that was more for movement than behavior. She felt this because the head turned toward her, and even though the eyes watching her were glass, she could see a spark of something behind them.

Awareness.

Bloody hell, this was not good.

"Why am I here?" Emily demanded of the...*thing*. She had no idea what to call it, but she knew not to underestimate it.

It clicked and clacked toward her, surprisingly nimble. Fast. It was horrifying, but she wasn't afraid. She was disturbed, perhaps even disgusted by it. It was no longer in its original design. Someone or something had modified it.

"You are here because you are needed," it replied. Its speech was slightly halting and a little rough, sounding as though it came from the bottom of a metal drum. "You are awake and dressed. You will come with me."

It was only when Emily opened her mouth to respond that she realized the machine had not spoken to her in English. It had spoken to her in a chittering, clicking manner, that somehow she understood.

She didn't attempt to respond in the same language, however. "I'm not going anywhere with you. Not until I know why I was taken from my home and am being treated like a prisoner."

The doll head cocked to one side—disconcerting. "You are a guest."

"Guests aren't coshed over the head and locked up in a dirty cell."

"This is all there is. The door is locked to protect you, protect us. You will come with me now, please?"

So it had some manners. That didn't make her feel any better than realizing she understood it had. "No."

One of the long legs reached out, the pincers at the end grabbing at her arm. Emily wrapped her fingers around it, reached deep down inside herself and called up her talent.

"What...what are you doing?" the spider demanded, its many limbs pumping and twitching as she forced her will upon it.

It was like she melded with the metal. Its energy flowed from metal to her skin, along her nerves to her brain, where something was able to process it all into information she could understand. Her skin tingled and her blood rushed through her veins, roaring in her ears. It was like being on the back of Sam's velocycle when he used to take her for drives and go as fast as the machine would move. She could almost feel the wind in her hair. It was exhilarating.

"You're going to let me go," Emily informed the

metal monster. "You are going to lead me out of here and let me go home. Understood?"

"Yes. No. That is not my mission."

"What is your mission?"

"I will not tell you. You cannot make me!"

The thing had her there. She was pushing her mind against it as hard as she could, but it was like trying to shove her brain out her nose. Even more worrisome was just how flimsy her hold on the ugly thing really was. If it was just a machine she could control it, but it was sentient and had free will.

It fought back. The pounding in her head and nausea in her stomach intensified, but she pushed harder. So did the machine.

A stab of pain exploded behind her eyes, white-hot and sharp, like being stabbed with a blade fresh from the forge.

She released the metal appendage, dropping her attempt at control like a hot iron. Immediately, the pain in her head lessened.

The doll head couldn't change its painted smile, but there was wariness in the eyes. She knew the feeling. Griffin's aunt Cordelia was a telepath. She'd dipped into Emily's brain once and never did again. Emily's reaction to the violation had been...indignant rage was probably the best description. She doubted Cordelia had felt the same sort of pain.

"Come with me."

Said the spider to the fly, Emily thought, massaging her forehead with her fingers. She followed after the skittering creature without argument. There might be a chance to escape, and at the very least she'd be able to better study her surroundings and get an idea of where she was. Once she knew that, she could figure out the best way to escape—or to get word to Sam and the others.

Sam. They hadn't gotten to finish their conversation.

That was what really pissed her off, to borrow a phrase from Finley. She should be back at King House listening to Sam tell her he loved her, too. At least, that was what she expected he might say—if he even realized that he loved her. And he had to love her, because seeing his face every day was what made her get out of bed some mornings, especially after a night of bad dreams.

Regardless of whether or not he was aware of his feelings, *she* knew that Sam would come for her. And she knew that Finley would be with him, and so would Griffin even though he was sick. And Jasper, despite his own problems, would come as well, because that's what friends did for one another. Her friends would soon be looking for her—if they weren't already.

She just had to stay alive long enough to be saved or save herself.

As the automaton led her away from her room, down a hall to another, larger space, Emily realized where she was. Underground, the catacombs. She knew because she could smell the hot grease from the trains on the steam-dampened air, and there was a bit of a Roman wall sticking up from the dirt floor. This might have been a street or an alley several centuries earlier.

Now it was home to a motley bunch that dropped her jaw as soon as she saw them.

Automatons. At least a dozen of them in various shapes and sizes and made from different materials. Some looked new, others ancient, and some had been patched together with scrap like old soldiers mended as best they could be on the field of battle and then sent home.

"How did you all come to be here?" she asked as, one by one, the machines stopped what they were doing and turned to her. Some were big and faceless things— nothing humanoid about them at all. Others were small and looked like dustbins or toys. A few were quite human, indeed.

There was another girl there. A pretty girl who looked vaguely familiar to her. Had they met before? Emily opened her mouth to say something, anything to get the girl's attention, and then quickly snapped it shut as the girl turned her head.

This was not a girl—not a human one at any rate. Not yet. She was lovely with hair much similar in color to Emily's own, but she was taller with more curves. Bits of her metal skeleton were still visible, though just barely through the pale flesh that covered her. She was being taken over by organic material, becoming a living thing.

And when she was done no one would know she wasn't human. This was the "package" Jack Dandy had been asked to deliver, she was sure of it. She was more organic now than when Jack had opened the crate, but it was her.

It wasn't coincidence that the machines had come for her, Emily realized, the notion taking hold with an icy certainty in the pit of her stomach. They had seen her with Finley earlier. Those feelings of having been watched were justified and not just paranoia. And certainly not rats. They had tracked her and brought her here, but why? Why her and not Finley?

The automaton led her into yet another room. A few

of the others followed. She could hear them chattering behind her—some in English, some in machine-speak. She understood some of it, but with all of them talking at once she could only pick out a few words like *mother, savior* and *master.* None of those were particularly comforting.

"This is why you are here," the metal told her, pointing one tarnished, arachnid-like limb at what appeared to be a large incubator. Emily turned her attention toward the glass tube setting in an iron base, tubes and wires running into and around it. A bellows kept the rhythm of relaxed human breathing.

When she saw what was in the tub she gasped. Horror grabbed her by the throat and squeezed hard.

"You will fix him, mother," the spider told her. "Fix our Master so that he may lead us."

Like hell she would. Fear bled away to rage. And hate.

It was Leonardo Garibaldi in that glass womb, the man responsible for the deaths of Griffin's parents and Finley's father. The man who would have killed them all if he could. The man whose experiments led to Sam's injuries.

"Like hell I'll fix him," she said. She'd die first.

Then there was a pinch in her arm. She turned

around to see the pretty automaton girl standing beside her, a syringe in her hand.

Then Emily's knees gave out and everything went
black.

Even Jasper joined the search for Emily. He took
off faster than a human could ever imagine, running
through the grounds and the entire neighborhood. Sam
checked her laboratory—again—and tried to reach her
on her portable telegraph.

The machine was on Emily's workbench in the
greenhouse, where Finley found it while searching the
building her friend had been taken from. Sam had already been through it, but he asked her to look, too.

"I don't trust my own judgment," he told her, fists
clenched. "I'm too angry and I'm too scared, and I don't
mind admitting it, not when it could make the difference between finding Em and not."

It was an oddly lengthy bit of conversation coming
from him. And she felt for him—sympathized even.

Whoever took Emily had hurt her. The blood on
the floor and splattered on a nearby plant was proof of
that. No wonder Sam didn't trust himself to be thorough. The thought of someone doing violence against
her friend woke up that part of her Finley thought long

gone, or at least long assimilated. It was her, but not her, and it wanted blood of its own.

She couldn't give in. She wouldn't. Out of all of them Emily was the most fragile. Finley knew it wasn't fair, but how could she not think that way? Next to Sam, Finley was the strongest of them all physically; Jasper could shoot the wings off a fly before you could blink; and Griffin could topple buildings. Emily could control machines but had no idea the extent of that ability. Unless she had some of her inventions with her she would have nothing but her wits to fall back on.

Emily was a bloody genius, but her brain couldn't rip the face off someone trying to hurt her.

Her automaton cat sat nearby. The cat should have protected Emily as it was programmed to do, but someone had yanked the power cell out of its chest panel. Poor thing. If it had been like Garibaldi's machines it might have defended itself, but it could only do what it was told. That was probably a good thing given that it had metal fangs—why Emily would install those was beyond her—and weighed more than a full-grown man.

Finley replaced the cell and the metal shield that went over it. In a few seconds the cat's eyes lit up and its engine engaged. She peered into its glowing gaze. Emily had placed something she called "optical aperture sensory devices" in the cat's head so that it could record what it saw. Maybe it had "seen" Emily's attackers before they disabled it.

She rose to her feet and studied the ground. There was no blood except for that one spot, which she assumed to be Emily's. No broken glass, no sign of a struggle. There were, however, little pits in the floor, as though something heavy and pointed had dug into it. There was also a set of footprints. Whoever left them had a heavy, shuffling gait.

"Find anything?" Sam stood at the threshold, as though he was afraid to enter the building, or was perhaps a vampire who had not been invited in, like in Mr. Stoker's book. After the past six months Finley wouldn't be surprised to find out such monsters truly existed.

Finley rose to her feet. "Maybe. Some interesting prints."

"I noticed those. Any idea what might have made those indents?"

"None. But I think the cat might have seen the kidnappers."

His dark eyes brightened. "Yeah? Let's take a look." He crossed the threshold and the distance between them in a few long strides, and scooped the metal feline up under his arm. She had to admit—but only to herself and never to him—that his strength was impressive.

"Do you know how to operate it?" he asked as they walked back to the house.

She shook her head. "Not really. I can flick the power switch. Griffin will know." Was there anything Griffin couldn't do as far as she was concerned?

A dull flush crept up Sam's cheeks. "About earlier…"

Finley held up her hand. "Please don't. I'd rather pretend it didn't happen." But it had. He had walked in at the worst possible moment and she didn't know whether to kill him or thank him for it. She wanted to be with Griffin in…*that* way, but she wanted him to feel as though he could confide in her first.

"You care about him—Griffin—don't you?"

The finer art of subtlety was obviously lost on him. A girl would have known she didn't want to talk about her relationship with Griffin. "Sam—"

"She told me she loves me."

Finley swallowed her words. If he'd dropped the cat on her foot she wouldn't have been more surprised. "What?"

His cheeks were crimson. "Em. Earlier today. She told me she loves me."

Emily O'Brien was the bravest person she'd ever

known. Quite possibly fearless. She was Finley's bloody hero. "What did you say?" It was none of her business, but she didn't know what else to say, and he was the one who had brought it up.

"Nothing." His jaw clenched as his gaze fell from hers. "Jasper showed up and I had to leave."

"What would you have said if Jasper hadn't come in when he did?"

Sam looked up, just barely making eye contact once more. "That I was the luckiest git in the world."

Finley smiled. She didn't often feel affection toward Sam, but this moment might change all that. "You are, indeed."

He frowned—it was a pained expression rather than his usual anger. The anguish in his eyes was almost too much, too personal, for Finley to bear. "What if...what if I never get to tell her?"

How the devil did this insufferable arse manage to break her heart so bloody easily? Her throat actually tightened.

"You'll be able to tell her, Sam. I promise you that. Now let's go find Griffin and see what our feline friend has to show us."

He nodded and fell into step beside her as they neared the house.

"Finley?"

Just over the threshold, she turned. "Yes?"

"Just so you know, Griffin cares about you, too. He wouldn't... He's not the kind of bloke that takes advantage. He has the most honor of anyone I know."

Did he realize, she wondered, that sometimes a girl didn't want honorable? That sometimes a girl wanted to be thoroughly kissed and swept off her feet? That sometimes girls wanted the same thing boys did? Had the same desires and needs? Probably not, because Sam Morgan was the kind of fellow who would lie down and die for the girl he loved but did not know how to actually voice his feelings.

So Finley merely nodded. "Thanks." It really didn't matter—not at that moment. Her feelings for Griffin and his feelings for her were the least of her concerns. Even his strange affliction came second to finding Emily. Nothing mattered more than bringing her best friend home again.

Nothing.

Chapter 7

"Are you broken?"

Emily turned her head toward the voice. Low and throaty, it was unfamiliar to her yet somehow comforting. She opened her eyes and found the automaton girl watching her. Well, she opened one eye; the other one took a little convincing, as it was on the battered side of her face.

The spider punched like a champion pugilist, wanker. Now her face hurt. At least her head felt better. "No. I don't think I'm broken, at least not in any way that can't be fixed." She lay back against the pillows—they had brought her back to her "cell" to wake up. "What's your name?"

"I'm called Endeavor 312." The girl—Emily couldn't think of her as a thing—moved closer, crouched on the floor by her bed. "You are the mother."

She frowned. "No, I'm not."

In return, 312 cocked her head, perplexed. "Yes, you are. Your genetic material is inside my own. You speak to metal, understand it. You are our mother."

"My genetic material…" Damnation. The warehouse where they'd taken on the Machinist. All of them would have left bits of themselves behind—blood, skin, hair. All the organites needed was a little piece of a person to copy their cellular structure. No wonder 312 looked so familiar—she was made up from bits of her, Finley, Jasper, Sam and Griffin. Not only was she a sentient machine on the verge of becoming almost completely human, there was a very good chance she might exhibit one, if not all, of their talents. She might even develop some of her own.

And she was at the whim of that awful spider creature. That was almost as disconcerting and frightening as the fact that the Machinist was not only alive but close by. He had to be in deplorable condition to require such treatment. Could he communicate with them at all? Of course they would protect him, try to save him. If she was their "mother," because she could speak to them then Leonardo Garibaldi was their father, because he had literally given them life by using the organite power source to power their logic engines.

That was a thought that made her want to be physically ill, and it wasn't all because of the concussion. This…girl could prove to be the most dangerous and powerful creature in Europe, perhaps the world, and she was at the control of a madman. Or, at least at the control of a madman's creations.

Brilliant.

"Are you supposed to guard me?" she asked. "Make sure I don't try to escape or anything?"

Endeavor 312—a horrid name—tilted her head to one side, so like Griffin often did. "Why would you want to leave? You have a design. You share in our purpose."

Whenever anyone began talking about purpose, design, fate, destiny—all that rubbish—Emily immediately began looking for an out. Life was not preordained. Life was not "God's plan." She knew this because no god, no matter Catholic, Protestant or any other denomination, would ever, ever, plan for her to have been raped and suffer as she had.

But, despite that, she kept a calm facade—not too

difficult when you were simply trying to keep from puking your guts up. "What purpose would that be?"

The girl watched her warily. She had no eyelashes around her left eye, which was the same color as Finley's, and one ear was slightly smaller than the other. The organites hadn't finished fleshing her out.

"I'm not supposed to talk about it."

Emily put on a sweet smile. "Oh, but you can tell me. I am the mother after all." When the girl didn't immediately respond, she tried another tactic. "I think you should have a proper name."

Amber eyes brightened. That "naked" lid was so odd. "Really?"

"Of course. Every girl has to have a name. You are a girl, aren't you?"

"Almost." Her childlike earnestness made Emily's heart pinch. "They tell me my systems are now at ninety-five percent human."

"Then you shouldn't have a machine name anymore. What would you like to be called?"

"Emily?" She suggested, expression hopeful.

Emily chuckled despite the danger of her circumstances. "You don't want my name, you want your own. Why don't you think about it?"

"I will." A pause. "You are a very nice person. I've only met one other person. He was very handsome."

"Long dark hair, dark eyes?"

The girl reached out and grabbed Emily's arm. "You know him?"

She could have broken the bone, but her grip was surprisingly gentle. "I do. He told me about you. His name is Jack Dandy."

"Jack Dandy." The name was wrapped in such a sigh it bordered on ridiculous. "See, you *are* part of the plan. Jack Dandy was supposed to see me so that we might find you."

With a portion of 312's genetic material made up from Emily's own, Emily had no doubt that this extraordinary creature could have found her regardless of Dandy's involvement. She didn't say that, however.

"If all of this has been part of a grand design, then don't you think it would be all right for you to tell me how I fit into the plan?"

The girl had a brain—or at least part of one. Without an examination that would require cutting through the scalp and removing a section of the metal that made up her skull, there was no way to tell just how formed that organ was. Regardless, she was not stupid. She might, however, be just naive enough to be manipulated. Taking advantage of someone was wrong, but Emily would make an exception in this case.

The Machinist was alive. She had to repeat it silently to herself just so she'd believe it. She had to get word to Griffin. Had to get home to her friends so they could prepare, take action.

Did Sam miss her? How could she have told him she loved him? Why had Jasper shown up at that moment?

"...listening."

Emily's head jerked up. "Hmm? I'm sorry, what did you say?"

The girl—thinking of her as a machine felt wrong — scowled petulantly. "I said you weren't listening to me."

"No, I'm afraid I wasn't. Sorry. My face really hurts, and I'm hungry."

"I can find you food. I don't know what to do about your head. What does *hurt* mean?"

"It means it feels really bad. Painful."

"Oh, *pain.*" Gorgeous eyes widened. Good Lord, she had eyelashes now on her left eye. They weren't as long and thick as the ones on her right eye, but they would be. Incredible. In the course of this brief conversation, she had become visibly more human. She would be fascinating to study. "I do not know how to cure pain."

If only she had some of her organites Emily would

be able to heal herself with a little salve. The "wee beasties"—as she called the organites—were in her blood and would heal her on their own, but it would take a little longer than applying them directly to the wound. Still, she'd be all right soon enough.

Provided no other bad-tempered machines decided to slap her.

"I'll be fine. Tell me again what you were saying. I promise to listen this time."

Although 312 looked dubious, she complied. "I said that Her Majesty had come up with a plan that will return our father to us so that he may lead us as was intended."

Her Majesty? Prickles of ice formed in her veins. "That's the Queen Victoria automaton, isn't it?"

"Automatons do not think. Do not feel. Automatons are machines. Her Majesty is *not* a machine." She sounded—and scowled—like Sam.

"Part of her is," Emily reminded her. "Just like part of you is machine."

The girl lashed out. Emily ducked to avoid yet another head injury, but she grabbed the very, very strong hand that swung just millimeters from her face. Every part of her had but one agenda—self-preservation. Emily's determination to not only survive, but to triumph was like a fire raging inside her, so it was no surprise when her talent screamed to the surface.

And the part of this nameless girl that was still machine answered the call. Her logic engine hadn't taken over completely just yet. There was still a good part of her that was far from human, never mind her "systems" being almost one hundred percent such. Before she could react, Emily had forced her to calm down.

"Get out of my head," 312 demanded, jaw tight. That was another part of her that was like Finley, who hated it when Cordelia tried to do a "reading" on her.

Emily continued to hold on. Soon she would be forced to let go, but for now she could make her point. "I'm not in your head. I'm in your logic engine. Humans don't have logic engines, only machines do."

And suddenly it made sense why Sam was so obsessed with the thought of no longer being human—because humans didn't have mechanical hearts, though some had metal grafted to their bones, or artificial limbs. The only difference was that Sam's arm was not just metal, but also flesh and blood and muscle, and his mechanical heart had been taken over by the organites so that there was real human tissue there.

One good jerk, and Emily was empty-handed. A

sharp stinging filled her palm, and she looked down to see blood seep out of a shallow tear. Blast.

On the floor a few feet away, 312 sat, legs splayed. Her trousers were old and shabby and ripped at the knee, and her shirt was two sizes too big. Had they dressed her in someone's castoffs? She might dress shabbily, but she looked like a warrior priestess, ready to rip Emily's head from her shoulders.

"I'm *not* a machine."

Emily shrugged. "You're not human, either. Not yet, otherwise my touch wouldn't have worked on you."

For a split second, she thought the girl might take another swing at her, and Emily poised to duck, but no strike came. The girl lowered her arm. She looked as though she had just eaten something bad. Did she even eat yet?

"Then that's my destiny, to become human. It makes sense. I would have to become human to complete my path."

Again the mention of destiny—not good. "Why is that?"

"Because I'm to help you save the Master." She seemed to have forgotten that she wasn't supposed to tell. This was not a surprise to Emily. The transfer of metal, gears, cogs and Aether to flesh, blood and muscle was not easy. Things were taken over, given new jobs, or destroyed if necessary. A logic engine did not function in the same manner as a human brain, though it did possess a memory. As the thing in her skull became more of a brain and less of an engine she would lose more and more memories of being a machine.

"You're going to insert part of his brain into the logic engine of my physical form. You will do this or we will put all of his brain into you."

Emily wasn't about to die for the Machinist. She wasn't going to allow anyone to die for him; nor was she going to allow him to live. She didn't know what to do about this machine that was rapidly evolving into a real girl, but she knew exactly what to do about Leonardo Garibaldi.

All she had to do was destroy his brain. All she had to do was commit murder.

Discovering what the cat "saw" was more difficult than Finley imagined it would be. First, they took the cat to the library, and then they had to wait a few moments for Griffin and Jasper to find them. Then, Griffin had to make adjustments to the cat because of the damage it had sustained protecting Emily. Griffin was somewhat mechanically minded, but not like Emily, so it took longer than it normally would have. His weakened state dragged it out even more.

Their group didn't function all that well if one of them was missing, Finley realized. She didn't say it aloud, because it didn't need to be said. The blokes were thinking the same thing, she was sure of it.

While Griffin tinkered, Finley went to the closest wall of leather-bound books and reached up for a pull-cord dangling from a bar just above her head. She tugged on the satiny rope and drew out a wide length of silk from the bar above. This screen was the canvas upon which they would watch what the cat projected. Then, she moved chairs around so that they could sit and watch.

It wasn't hard work by any stretch of the imagination, but it gave her something to do other than stare at Griffin and wonder if he regretted the interruption of their earlier encounter as much as she did.

And was he as relieved by it as she was? She wanted him more than anything else. Wanted his heart and his trust so badly her chest ached with it. That kind of emotion and neediness frightened her. What if they tried to have a relationship and it failed? What if she wasn't good enough for him? One voice in her head said they had absolutely zero chance of having any kind of future, while another whispered that Griffin was a duke and he could do whatever he wanted. If he wanted her then they could make it work.

But she knew that men of his station often became bored with women, and had mistresses as well as a wife—not that she wanted to be Griffin's wife. She didn't want to be anyone's wife, not at that moment. She was of marriageable age, but there were a lot of things she wanted to do and see before she became some man's property and baby-making machine.

Not like that was necessarily going to happen. She'd either have to marry someone like herself, or someone she could trust with her secret. And then they would have to discuss children. She could pass on her abilities to a child, as could the father. That was a lot of responsibility.

So was protecting the Empire, and she didn't do that all by herself.

She turned her head to look at Griffin. He was the finest fellow she had ever laid eyes on. He was so beautiful it sometimes hurt to look at him. He was talking to Sam, but she didn't care what he was saying—she just wanted to admire him.

Sam brought the cat over beside her and set it down. Finley's gaze caught Griffin's. He stared at her for a moment—a long, breathtaking moment—before offering her a small, intimate smile. Her stomach fluttered.

"You reckon the cat saw the weasels who took Miss Emmy?" Jasper asked her.

Reluctantly, Finley turned away from Griffin's warm gaze. "I hope so. It would be helpful to have an image or face for the search."

"Why would anyone take her?" Sam asked. "Why Emily?"

"Why not?" Finley countered. "She's as useful as any of us."

He glared at her. "I know that, but would any of us have done, or did they target her especially?"

"I can't image a girl like her having enemies," Jasper said, halting the escalation of their conversation into a full-on fight. "The rest of us, sure, but Miss Emmy's a sweet girl, and a good person."

There was no offense in his voice, and Finley didn't take any. He was right—Emily was the best of all of them, and there was no reason for anyone to hurt her.

Unless it was to hurt one, or all, of them.

"We'll find her," Griffin assured them in his typical fashion. It wasn't just the bravado that came with being rich and titled—it was determination. He'd taken them to New York to help Jasper, and he wouldn't rest until they found Emily. "We'll find who took her."

"And rip them apart," Sam vowed. He rubbed his knuckles—knuckles that were metal beneath the skin. Finley agreed with him but didn't say it. She didn't need to—they were all thinking it. Emily meant so much to each of them, they would indeed kill for her.

Sam turned down the lamps, darkening the room and they each took a seat in front of the silk screen. Griffin positioned the cat just so and engaged its power cell. It purred to life, eyes lighting up. He adjusted the eye settings so that there would be one image on the screen—basically the right and left eyes overlapping—and flipped a series of small switches inside the control panel on the cat's side. Light hit the screen flickering and crackling. Then, an image appeared.

It was the greenhouse. Emily puttered about at her bench. Finley swallowed at the sight of her, smiling and happy. Emily looked up. There was someone else there. The figure drew closer.

"Is that…" Jasper blinked. "Is that the queen?"

Finley froze, saw Griffin and Sam stiffen. It was Queen Victoria, although not the real monarch.

"Damnation," Sam murmured.

The Queen Victoria automaton. Finley thought they'd seen the last of her when she'd popped her head off like the cork in a champagne bottle. They thought her destroyed. Obviously, they were wrong. What else had they been wrong about?

Another automaton came into view. This one was built like a man, but that was the end of his resemblance to humanity. It was made of brass, tarnished and dull. Its joints moved, but it had the stiff grace of a machine. It turned its blank face toward the cat. It had two sensors for eyes and a slit for a mouth. It had no expression whatsoever, but Finley could sense its intent.

The brass man moved toward Emily. Finley held her breath, even though she knew what came next. They could only watch as their friend roused only to be struck hard on the head by the brass man's hand. Finley cringed. Poor Emily—she never saw it coming.

They watched as their friend was taken away by the disturbing-looking old woman, her head bent at a curious angle, and then the form of the brass man blotted out the rest of the room just seconds before the entire scene went black. That was it.

It was enough. Enough to ignite real fear in Finley's chest. "Do you think…"

"We have to assume," Griffin said as he powered down the cat. His gaze didn't quite meet hers.

"Garibaldi's alive?" Sam's brows actually lifted momentarily. "Isn't that a stretch? How could he have survived that building collapse?"

"I don't know." Griffin shook his head. "But he did. It all makes sense."

Something in his tone caught Finley's attention. She opened her mouth to ask him what made sense, but Jasper cut her off. "So, what do we do now? Assumin' the Machinist is alive and that he has her, we have no idea where he'd be squirreled up, and no idea if he plans to keep her or pick us off one by one."

"If he was going to kill her he would have done it here." Griffin's tone was as dark and grim as his expression. "He'd leave her for us to find."

"You seem certain of that," Jasper commented.

Griffin shrugged. "I know him."

"How?" Finley couldn't stop the question from leaping from her mouth. "You barely met him. If any of us would have an idea of how his mind works, it's Sam." Sam had been manipulated by the madman into thinking him a friend.

Sam nodded. "Griff's right. If he planned to kill Em, Garibaldi would've wanted us to have the horror of finding her. If he is the one who took her, then he wants her for something else. Probably to get to you." His gaze settled on Griffin.

Finley's heart thumped hard. The thought of losing Griffin terrified her even more than the idea of losing Emily. She would not let Garibaldi have him.

"I have no doubt that the scoundrel wants to drive me mad," Griffin replied, a grim set to his mouth.

"You talk like you are certain it's him." Finley regarded him carefully. "But you can't be certain, not yet. None of us can."

Griffin looked as though he wanted to argue with her but held back the urge. What wasn't he saying? "Until we determine differently, I think we must assume Garibaldi is alive. Prepare for the worst and hope we're wrong."

She arched a brow, and didn't care that he saw it. She knew Griffin was hiding something, and if it pertained to Emily and her safety that was wrong of him. Wrong and potentially dangerous.

He turned away. "I need to check the security stations around the house. The automatons didn't trigger any alarms and I don't like that."

"I'll come with you," Jasper offered. "If somethin' needs repairing I can do it right quick."

That left Finley with Sam—normally not a brilliant combination.

"What's wrong with him?" Sam asked, jerking his chin toward the door after Griffin and Jasper walked out it."

"I don't know, but it worries me."

"You're worried about him."

"Of course I am, but right now I'm more worried about Emily." Despite her suspicions, she knew Griffin would not do anything to endanger one of his friends. If he wasn't telling them something, it was because he wanted to be certain before he said anything.

Although he had jumped pretty darn quick on the idea of Garibaldi being alive.

"Yeah. I reckon that's the one thing you and I have in common—we both care about Em."

She gave him a small smile. "And we both have naturally charming dispositions."

His lips curved a little at her sarcasm. "That, too." He ran a hand over the back of his neck. "You think Dandy might know if Garibaldi's back?"

"He might. He might also be able to find out about the automatons."

"Maybe that one he delivered was one of 'em."

Normally Finley might take that as a bit of a jump in logic, but not right then. "Emily and I went into the catacombs where Jack delivered the crate. It felt like we were being watched, even though we didn't find any evidence of automatons."

Sam's face adopted an expression of puzzlement rather than anger. "You'd have to have seen some evidence of automatons. They use them to patrol the underground, clean the sewers and catch rats. There'd be tracks everywhere."

"There weren't."

"Then someone covered them up. Come on, let's go."

"To the catacombs?"

"No, to Dandy's. We go stomping around underground. They'll see us and know we're onto them. I'm not rushing in like a damn fool and getting Emily hurt."

She actually drew up short. "Look at you being all logical."

He chuckled. "Logic has nothing to do with it. I want to tear the underground apart until I find her. She'd be the one wanting to gather all the facts." The smile slid from his face. "I...I need to find her, Finley. I want to be the kind of man she deserves."

Never in a million years would she have thought he'd confess that, especially not to her. "Then I guess we'd better find her so you can start deserving her. Get going then. Even Jack Dandy sleeps."

Chapter 8

Jack Dandy lived in Whitechapel, quite a bit east of Griffin's house in Mayfair. In fact, two parts of the city couldn't be more opposite each other than Mayfair and Whitechapel. Mayfair was clean and pretty with ladies and gentlemen dressed in the highest of fashions driving expensive steam carriages and mechanical horses, and servants to take care of them all. Whitechapel was gray and sooty with coal smoke. Men and women dressed in colors that matched the area so the dirt didn't show quite so much. Real horses, thin and old, hauled carts of precious fruit that none from the area could afford. Other wagons held prisoners bound for Newgate or Old Bailey.

It was here, one decade ago, that Jack the Ripper roamed the night, murdering prostitutes in a most horrible fashion. Rumor had it that Griffin's family had been instrumental in ending the Ripper's reign of terror, making certain he never hurt anyone again. What would Griffin's parents think of him kissing a girl who felt perfectly safe on the streets of Whitechapel? A girl who held a criminal as one of her closest friends?

Then again, perhaps Griffin already knew what they thought. His ability to manipulate Aether, to see it, also gave him the ability to see ghosts, so perhaps the late duke and duchess had already informed him of their opinion. They'd known her father. Known about the experiments that made his personality split into a good half and a dark half.

Finley shook her head as she and Sam approached the door of Jack's home. Now was not the time to be worrying about the dead. Emily mattered more than her personal life at the moment.

"That one." She pointed at the town house door. "That's Jack's."

Sam gestured for her to precede him up the shallow steps. Finley rapped her knuckles hard against the heavy door that was painted a deep, dark red.

"Can't be much money in crime," Sam remarked, looking about their surroundings.

Finley gave him a look. "Appearances are sometimes deceiving."

The door opened. On the other side of it was Jack, clad in a black silk dressing gown. It was open at the neck, giving her an eyeful of his naked, muscular chest. She couldn't help but stare. No girl alive would be able to resist that temptation.

"Are you done objectifyin' me, Treasure?" he asked drily. "I don't mind, o' course, but I don't fancy 'aving all of Whitechapel taking a gander at me ankles. A bloke 'as to 'ave some secrets, right?"

She should be embarrassed, but with Jack she felt none of that. That was how she knew that no matter how pretty he was, or how muscular his chest and calves were, she would never feel the same way about him that she did about Griffin.

"Can't blame a girl for looking, Jack," she retorted, and stepped in around him.

Jack raised a brow at Sam. "Might as well come on in, too, mate. I know she won't be leavin' until she gets what she come for."

"I won't keep you from your beauty rest for long, Jack," Finley shot back as she strode into the drawing room. She loved that room with its dark wood and deep red fabrics. It looked more like something from a high-class bordello than someone's home—not that she had much experience with bordellos.

"I should 'ope not, luv. It takes a lot of rest to be this gorgeous." He went straight to the bar, bare feet silent on the carpet. "Can I gets you anyfing?"

"Just some information," Finley replied, plopping down on the sofa. Sam sat down at the other end, and for a second, she felt her side lift. How much did he bloody weigh? Or was it the tension in his metal-enforced legs that created the imbalance?

"What about you, goliath?" Jack asked, pouring a measure of whiskey into a glass. "Anyfing to wet your whistle?"

"No, thank you."

"Ah, now there's some politeness, some manners. Observe this fellow, Treasure. Observe and learn the finer art of deportment."

Sam grinned. Finley was so stunned by the transformation that she forgot to be miffed. So *that* was what Emily saw whenever she looked at Sam. She saw that smile. She had to admit, he wasn't bad to look at when he smiled.

"Right," she drawled. "Jack dearest, our friend Emily has disappeared. She's been abducted."

He came around from behind the bar to seat himself in a wing-back chair. The crimson velvet contrasted richly with the black silk of his robe. "What, the little ginger? What sort of villain would 'urt that sweet bird?"

Finley cast a glance at Sam, but he didn't seem the least bit perturbed to hear Jack describe Emily in that fashion. "She was taken by automatons. One of them was built by the Machinist."

Jack's angular brows pulled together. "I thought you lot brought a buildin' down on 'is 'ead."

"We did," Sam replied before she could. "I don't think it took."

Their host took a sip of his whiskey. "Right. 'Ad that 'appen a few times meself. Some blokes you got to hit with something a bit 'arder than a roof."

Finley did not want to know. Well, maybe she did, but if she asked, Jack might actually tell her some of the things he'd done, and she wasn't certain she really wanted to know that side of him. It was one thing to think he was dangerous and another to know where the bodies were buried.

"He wasn't found in the rubble," Sam explained. "We

thought a couple of the automatons took what was left of him away, but perhaps he survived."

"And you think a couple of 'is metal took your lady-love." *Metal* was a slang term applied to automatons in general.

Sam actually blushed—poor lamb. "We know that one of them was his. It was the very one you found on your step."

"The one what looked like Her Nibs?" At Sam's nod, Jack started laughing. "On my step in 'er unmentionables, she were. Not something you can unsee, right? Resemblance was uncanny. Right, so you want to know if I've 'eard anyfing that might be useful?"

"Exactly," Finley replied. "So, have you?"

Another drink. "Not sure, luv. Aside from my dealings, I've 'eard of a few incidents that involved metal as of late. Some petty theft, procurement. Weird stuff, too, like medical equipment and assorted potions from the chemist."

Finley and Sam exchanged a glance. "Those sort of things would come in handy if you had a wounded human to attend."

Sam nodded. "They'd need some place large and private to keep him. Like underground."

That led to another question. "When you delivered

the crate to St. Pancras station, do you remember seeing signs of automaton traffic?"

Jack looked at her as though she was mentally deficient. "'Course. Were tracks all over the place. Though, I did see a little one—one of those sweepers—tidying up. I assumed that was just more of our taxes being put to good use."

She gave him an arch look. "You expect me to believe you pay taxes?"

"Of course I pay me taxes. I'm a law-abidin' citizen. I want to keep Her Nibs in comfort, same as everyone else."

"*Riiight.* So, I'd like you to come into the tunnels with us and show us the spot."

"It was the platform, and no, I won't come wiv you."

"Why not?" Indignation kept her from wincing as her voice went up an octave. Jack was refusing her? Now of all times?

"Because it won't do to have them what I've done business with seeing me wiv you. Sorry, Treasure, but I've a reputation to fink of."

"Your reputation is more important than Emily?" She couldn't keep the disbelief from her voice.

Jack raised one brow ever so slightly as his gaze locked with hers. "That's right. My apologies if that stings, but it's the way of it. This side of town if a man don't 'ave 'is reputation, 'e ain't got nothin'.'"

That was a great, steaming pile of…

"He's right," Sam said. He looked at Jack as though he understood him. "But I'm willing to bet you can give us the exact location."

Another sip of whiskey. "I can at that, my son. Marked it, in fact, as I often do in circumstances where I fink it might be 'elpful."

"Why didn't you tell us that before?" Finley demanded.

He turned on her with a dry expression. "Just because I adore you don't mean you get all my secrets, Treasure. I didn't think it was important at the time, now it is." He didn't apologize, just went on to tell Sam where to look. "Carved a *D* on the stone. Not terribly original, but does the trick. I'll keep me ears open, too, let you know if I 'ear anyfing about the Machinist or 'is metal."

Sam nodded. "Thanks."

"Jack?" came a voice from outside the room. "Is everything all right?"

Finley's head came up. Standing in the doorway was a beautiful woman, perhaps a few years older than Jack. She wore a purple velvet dressing gown that clung to her stunning figure, and had long curly black hair and flawless pale skin.

She was the kind of woman that inspired hate and feelings of inadequacy in other females, and she obviously wasn't there to play cards.

"It's all right, darlin'. Go back up. I'll be there shortly."

She smiled at him, a seductive smile that made Finley feel as feminine as Sam's left foot. The woman was a goddess. "All right." She wiggled her fingers at Sam and Finley. "Sorry to interrupt."

Finley stared after her. So did Sam. The only one of them who didn't seem enthralled by the woman was Jack. That didn't seem right, but it wasn't her place to judge. After all, she was the one who had knocked on his door without giving any thought to whether or not he was alone.

No, that was a lie. She had assumed he'd be alone. She'd assumed he'd be pleased to see her. She might not love him, but she liked his attention. Did that make her a horrible person? Perhaps it did, or perhaps it didn't. Right now it didn't matter.

"We should go," she said, rising to her feet. Suddenly things seemed awkward and odd, and they had more pressing things to do, such as finding Emily. "Jack, thank you for your help."

He also stood. "'Aven't done nuffing yet, but you're welcome. I'll let you know if I 'ear anyfing."

He led them to the door and held it open for them. Sam shook his hand and thanked him for his time, then crossed the threshold out into the night. Finley hung back for a moment.

"I'm sorry we intruded upon your...visit," she said, forcing herself to meet his gaze. "Why did you even answer the door?"

"You know why. I'll always answer for you, Treasure."

She nodded. "I hope I never take your friendship for granted, Jack."

He allowed a little smile. "You let me worry about that, luv. You worry about finding your little bird. Now, out you go. Back to Mayfair to your charming duke."

Was he mocking her? It didn't matter. "Bye, Jack." She stepped out into the waning day.

The door clicked shut behind her. Finley wasn't certain how she should feel at that moment, so she chose to be hopeful. "Come on," she said to Sam, who was watching her. "Let's go home."

★ ★ ★

The thought of committing murder didn't weigh as heavily on Emily's shoulders as it should have. In fact, she was much more angry than scared. If the Machinist had just had the good manners to die when Griffin brought that building down on him none of this would be happening. She would not be plotting how to end Garibaldi without getting herself killed.

But putting that diabolical brain into a young, almost indestructible body that could have incredible powers was not something she was going to do.

"I need to see what I'm working with," she told "Victoria," ignoring that awful bent neck.

The old woman assessed her, inner gears clicking. Something had happened to halt the automaton's progress to humanity. It had died when its head had been ripped off, and now it was a machine in a flesh suit. To an extent, the organites had kept the flesh and tissue from decaying but couldn't advance its evolution.

It was basically like dealing with a reanimated corpse.

"How do we know you won't harm the Master?"

"That wouldn't be logical of me, would it?" Machines understood logic and order—patterns. Trying to appeal to emotions would be useless, but facts were always easily computed. "If I harm your master, you'll harm me. That's not something I'd like to happen."

Another few seconds ticked by as the automaton's guts whirred and clacked. "No. Harming yourself would be illogical. We will show you what you wish to see. We will answer your questions so you will fix the Master."

Emily's shoulders sagged with relief. "Thank you." So far the morning was off to a smashing start. Earlier, after waking up determined to make it out of this situation alive, she'd managed to talk them into bringing her water so she could bathe and wash her hair. Her scalp ached and itched, but it felt divine to get rid of the blood. She also put on a fresh change of clothes from the selection of her own they'd brought with her. How had they gotten into the house?

All she had to do now was buy enough time to plot how to get herself out of this situation. She was prepared to kill if necessary, but she'd much rather free herself and come back with her friends than do it all on her own.

"Victoria" turned with a clunk of gears, then led the way out of the cell. Emily followed behind her, eyes taking in every detail of her surroundings. She noted every machine, every patched-together device and the pipes that ran steam throughout the compound. The air was moist and warm, with the slight chill that came from being underground.

An automaton that looked like a stick with long, thin arms and legs and a narrow, heart-shaped head soldered a patch onto a small, dingy machine with a cage in its midsection, and pincerlike hands designed to catch rats. A narrow-faced rodent peered out from the slender bars of the cage and squeaked. Emily shuddered and turned away. She'd never much cared for rats. They were sneaky creatures who, if backed into a corner, would fight like mad to save themselves.

Perhaps there was something to like about rats after all.

The machines watched as she went by. Some of them were still metal enough that she could reach out, touch them and have them do whatever she wanted. Good. That would be handy when the time came to get herself out of there. Hopefully they wouldn't evolve in the meantime to the point where her touch would be useless.

A brass man turned his head as she passed, face blank except for two "eyes" and a slash of a mouth. Those were the kind that unsettled her more than the realistic machines.

Finally they arrived at what Emily thought of as the laboratory—the room where Leonardo Garibaldi lay in a glass vat of viscous, life-sustaining fluid. She stood there a moment, studying the setup, trying to determine what part all the tubes and wires and mechanisms played in keeping this monster from an unmarked grave.

She didn't hate him just because he'd tried to kill them, or take over the empire. She didn't hate him for the fact that he had murdered Griffin's parents and played a hand in the death of Finley's father. No, Emily despised Garibaldi because he'd tried to use Sam. He'd traded on Sam's vulnerability and tried to turn him against his friends. Garibaldi had played him for a fool.

For that she could cheerfully pull all the wires out of the fluid bath and let him flop around like a beached fish.

But not yet.

Her gaze settled on the bellows that kept the Machinist breathing. Electrical current kept his heart beating and blood flowing. He was like a modern-day Frankenstein's monster.

She turned to the Victoria automaton in one last attempt to bargain with it. "What you're asking me to do is impossible. You can't just cut open a person's skull and muck about with their brain. I'm not a surgeon with years of experience. I could accidently kill him or destroy his mind."

"You speak falsehood, Emily O'Brien," the machine chastised. "We know about the procedure you performed on that boy in Ireland. You have 'mucked about' before."

Hot pinpricks raced through her veins. How could they know? He'd fallen from a tree, and was delivered to her house because the doctor was away. She told them she had to relieve swelling on his brain, and they believed her because she was educated and they didn't think sweet Emily O'Brien, whom they'd known her entire life, would lie.

But she had lied, just so she could make sure he never forced himself on another girl.

"I didn't remove parts of his brain and replace it with parts from another. You have to be certain of compatibility between the two patients."

"Endeavor 312 was designed to contain sufficient genetic material to be a suitable receptacle. The Master made certain of that."

That was a surprise. "So, Garibaldi—your master—began work on 312 before the warehouse incident?"

"Indeed. She was to be his finest creation—after me, of course."

"Of course." But Garibaldi couldn't know that the organites added to her genetic map. There might only be a small part of her creator left inside her, if any. Curiosity, or perhaps paranoia, made her ask, "What was her original intent?"

"To infiltrate the household of the Duke of Greythorne, learn his secrets and vulnerabilities."

Emily's heart skipped a beat even as her brow gave a dubious lift. "That's a lofty goal."

"The chance of success was calculated to be much higher than the chance of defeat. It no longer matters— her purpose has changed. She has been given a great honor."

Tell that to 312, the almost-girl who deserved a name rather than a number. Never mind that she'd snap Emily's spine like a twig if she tried to escape. No, 312 was as much a prisoner here as she was.

Though, Emily wasn't going to let empathy get in the way of saving herself. Making certain the Machinist did not succeed was top priority. Her own safety came second. If 312 came out of it with her own budding brain in her skull that would just be a plus. Emily would figure out what to do with her then.

"The liquid he's suspended in, what is it?"

A faint whirring came in response—the machine weighing whether or not it should share that information. "A compound derived from the organic material your kind refers to as organite, minerals, nutrients and amniotic fluid."

Disgusting, but brilliant. "How can you be certain his brain is intact? The injuries he sustained might have very well left him an invalid."

"Victoria" lifted her chin proudly. It only pronounced the disturbing angle of her crooked neck. "Thanks to the Master's designs we were able to construct a device to communicate with him via the Aether. We cannot do it often, but he is there." She stroked the tank containing her creator in a loving fashion. "He speaks to us. It was he who told us how to bring about his resurrection."

Resurrection? Faith and *begorra*. This man was no saint or savior, but it made sense that he was guiding his machines. Obviously all efforts were being put into keeping his brain as healthy as possible—to the further detriment of his body. The organites could heal just about anything, but even they had limits. They couldn't give life where there wasn't any, and Garibaldi hovered on the brink of death. The organites kept his blood flowing, but everything they did was for his brain. God only knows how advanced his mind was at this point, after months of organite exposure. If he managed to have a presence on the Aetheric plane he would be able to influence their logic engines and any signals they received. He'd be able to travel the Aether as a being of pure energy.

Griffin believed that the Aether was a place of souls—the energy of every creature who ever lived. It was everywhere, and even had its own dimension. A person needed only to know how to see it to traverse in it. Of course, Griffin could also channel that energy into raw power.

If she could only get a message to Griffin he could use his abilities to search the Aether for Garibaldi. He could stop this.

Of course there was no way to get a message to Griffin. She didn't have her portable telegraph, and even if she could find the necessary pieces to construct a new one, she didn't have the time.

Unless…unless she could figure out some way to contact Griffin through Garibaldi's Aetheric connection. It would be tricky—possibly endanger her life if the bounder alerted the machines to her perfidy—but it was a chance she had to take. She'd never thought of herself as particularly brave, but when she'd agreed to work for Griffin, she knew there could be consequences. That there could be real danger.

Still, she wanted to make a difference. She wanted to protect the weak and fight those who took joy in hurting others. Garibaldi was one of those sorts of people. So, as soon as she figured out how to do it, she'd contact Griffin and tell him where she was—to her best estimation. They'd find her.

"Here are our Master's notes, computations and designs." "Victoria" offered her a stack of journals almost a foot tall. "They will instruct you how to better understand the procedure. He was very successful with his own experiments in brain transplantation."

The man had no decency. Bad things came to those who tampered with Mother Nature, God, whatever you wanted to call the vast wonder that made up the world, the cosmos and life itself. She had no idea what else she might find in those papers. If she was lucky there would be something about Aetheric projection. Worst-case scenario, she would determine the precise way to sabotage Garibaldi's plans.

She took the papers—the pile was heavier than it looked. "I will begin reading immediately." Did she sound too keen?

"Victoria" nodded. At least it looked like she tried to nod. It really wasn't much more than an inch of forward motion from her neck and head. Just when Emily thought she might be getting used to the disturbing visage that was a horrific parody of the Queen of England, something else happened to remind her of just how terrifying it actually was.

"You will start reading now. You have two days to locate the correct procedure and begin work."

Two days? That was it? Wait. Two days to *locate* the procedure? "I thought you already found instructions within his notes?"

Whirl. Click. Crackle. Click. Click. Thin lips opened, moved. No sound came out except the sound of a logic engine working over a problem. Then, "We are programmed to learn, to adapt. We recognize numbers, logic. We can speak, but we have not learned to identify the written word."

Emily stared, jaw loose. "You can't read?" On one hand it made perfect sense that they wouldn't recognize letters and words. On the other, why the hell hadn't Garibaldi given them the ability through their logic engines? Maybe such complex work was outside his comprehension, or perhaps he thought he'd be around to teach them personally. Regardless, it was something she would use to her advantage if at all possible.

Meanwhile, she had a lot of reading to do if she was going to protect the world from the Machinist again. Maybe she'd get lucky and she wouldn't have to murder him at all.

Chapter 9

"You should have told me you were going to see Dandy."

Finley's hands went to her hips. He sounded jealous. "You were off checking the security system around the house. Besides, Sam was with me to make certain I didn't throw myself at Jack." It was shrewish and uncalled-for, and she was sorry the moment the words left her tongue.

Griffin scowled—he was becoming more and more like Sam every day and it wasn't attractive. "I'm not jealous, if that's what you're thinking."

"No?" She smiled at him. This was not going to escalate into a stupid fight just because they were both on edge. "Tell me honestly—are you more bothered by the fact that I didn't tell you where we were going, or the fact that it was Jack I went to see?"

He looked as though he'd rather eat worms than answer her. "The fact that it was Dandy. I see how he looks at you."

"There, that wasn't so hard, was it?" She arched a brow. "Maybe next you can tell me why you look like you haven't been eating or sleeping? What keeps you locked up in your rooms, passing out when you use your power and having mediums over for breakfast?"

Griffin's jaw set mulishly. "What bothers you more— the fact that I'm doing these things, or the fact that you don't know why?"

Leave it to him to throw her own childishness back in her face. "That I don't know why, of course."

She expected him to gloat a little or perhaps brush it off, but he did neither. "I won't share you, Finley. If you want to be friends with Dandy, fine, but you have to know that he doesn't want to be just friends."

"I know that," she replied. "I also know that he would never try to force the issue, and I know that Jack isn't going to waste time pining for me, either."

"Is that what you want?"

"This is ridiculous." She decided to borrow a page

from Emily's book, and go for complete honesty. It was the only way to stop this conversation from becoming more of a habit than it already was.

She walked up to him and placed her hands on either side of his face so he would be forced to look at her. "I might take Jack soup if he was ill, maybe even sit with him. I would not bathe him. I would not wash his hair, and when I look at him I do not think about kissing him." Impulsively, she traced the bow of his lower lip with her thumb. "There's only one mouth I think about kissing."

Griffin's gaze warmed beneath his heavy lids. He had a way of looking at a girl that made her want to toss propriety and virtue to the wind. "Whose mouth is that?" His voice was low and rough as his fingers hooked into the front lacing of her corset and pulled her closer.

"Yours, you great daft article. Not Jack's, only yours. Will you stop being jealous of him now?"

"He's rich, handsome and dangerous. You like that."

She smiled at the uncharacteristic lack of self-confidence in his tone. "My dear duke. *You* are rich, handsome and dangerous."

His lips lifted on one side. "I would never describe myself as dangerous."

"Could you maybe stop talking? I'd like to kiss you but your lips won't stay still."

Eyes twinkling, he pressed his lips shut. Finley smiled and guided his head down to hers.

Then, like a scene in a comedy—their lips but a breath away from touching—the door to the library burst open and Sam charged into the room like a bull, a map in his hands and Jasper hot on his heels.

Bloody hell, they had brilliant timing. She could've cheerfully strangled the pair of them—all three of them, really.

Sam didn't even appear to notice that he'd interrupted something—again. "I found the maps of the Metropolitan system and the catacombs." He used one big arm to wipe the desk completely clear of papers and unrolled the maps on the polished surface, oblivious to the debris floating to the floor around him.

Griffin shot Finley a glance. He looked annoyed to have been interrupted—as was she—but there was something there that told her he planned to continue their conversation later. She would make certain of it.

They gathered around the desk to look at Sam's findings. He pointed out the St. Pancras station where Jack had delivered the crate with the automaton.

"That station gets a lot of traffic," Griffin said, stating what Finley had already thought. "A crate couldn't just sit there for long."

"Jack said he left the letter *D* carved on the wall near the spot where he deposited the crate," she informed him. "Emily and I were in the catacombs, though. Not in the station."

Sam nodded and pointed to a spot on another map. It was a detailed drawing of the catacombs that noted London landmarks and metro stations. "This is the area around St. Pancras where you and Em were looking about."

"Is that a stairwell?" Jasper asked, leaning in for a closer look. When Finley and Griffin moved, their shoulders brushed and Finley's foolish heart gave a jump. Stupid thing.

Warm fingers entwined with hers, blocked from Jasper and Sam's view by the desk. She closed her hand around his.

"Exactly." Sam's finger slid over to the spot on the map. "This was one of the documents we managed to recover from Garibaldi's warehouse. It marks several underground stairwells and doors that link to other parts of the system but that aren't on any official maps."

Griffin glanced up. "Garibaldi constructed them?"

"Em thought so." Sam shrugged. "It makes sense. It

also stands to reason that the metal that almost killed me was one of Garibaldi's machines. He'd been using organites in his inventions, so it would explain the machine breaking its programming."

It did make sense, and if it was true then Sam had all the more reason to hate the Machinist.

"So you reckon whoever wanted the crate collected it from the station and then took it into the catacombs via Garibaldi's secret exits?" she asked.

Sam's gaze met with hers, confident and determined. "I do."

"It supports the theory that the Machinist is alive and behind this." Griffin's expression was suitably grim.

Finley frowned. "It could be someone who worked with him. Someone who knew him."

There was a pause, as though Sam and Jasper were wondering which theory to support.

"Finley's right," Sam said finally. "We shouldn't assume it's him until we have more proof."

"It sure seems like it might be him," Jasper added, surprising her by joining the conversation, "but I also have a hard time believin' he walked away from that building fallin' down around him. Besides, if it was the scoundrel, wouldn't he have sent word that he had Miss Emily by now? Seems he'd take some pleasure in letting you know he had her." He looked from Sam to Griffin—the two most important men in Emily's life.

Griffin's expression was tight. Finley felt for him—a little. He wasn't used to being questioned. He was a duke, after all. He was also decisive, perceptive and usually right. Still, it seemed his personal fears and feelings might be clouding his judgment. "Fine. We'll treat this as though it might not be Garibaldi, but that it may be related to him."

"You seem pretty keen on layin' this at the Italian's feet," Jasper commented. "Anythin' you want to share?"

Finley turned her gaze to Griffin to see his reaction, but he was staring at a point over Jasper's shoulder, his eyes and expression hard. "The three of you need to leave this room. Now."

What the devil? Finley followed his gaze. There was nothing there. "Griffin…"

"Finley, get out. *Now*." His jaw was clenched, face etched with something that looked like a combination of hate and fear.

"We're not going anywhere," she informed him, pointing a warning finger at Sam as he started gathering up the maps to do what he was told.

"I'm not going argue with you," Griffin ground out. "Get the hell out of this room."

Finley opened her mouth to disagree, but not a sound came out. Suddenly there was a terrible banding around her throat, cutting off her breath. She tried to suck in air, but it was impossible, and the invisible hands around her neck squeezed tighter.

Hands. Yes, it felt like hands. Her vision began to waver.

Griffin swore. Out of the corner of her eye, with what vision she had, she saw him grab Jasper by the arm. "Sorry, my friend, but I need your help with this, and I don't have time to explain."

Jasper blinked. "What the hell... Oh, no. No."

Finley gasped for air as she turned her gaze forward once more. Suddenly, as the world grew more narrow, she began to see a figure before her. Long black hair. Almond-shaped eyes. As her lungs strained for air, the face of her assailant became clearer.

It was Mei, the girl Jasper had once loved. The girl Griffin had accidentally killed. She glared at Finley with inky, iris-less eyes, a determined expression on her face.

Was she a ghost? She had to be—her own imagination wasn't nearly this powerful, and Griffin had seen her first.

Blackness invaded her vision. Finley grappled for

Mei's arms, but her fingers went right through them. Her form was as insubstantial as fog. Dimly, over the roaring in her ears, she heard Jasper speak. He was pleading with Mei, asking her to stop. And Griffin was reaching for her...

And that was it. The last thought Finley had as she sank into oblivion was how it would be just her luck to be murdered by a bloody ghost.

The sleeping beauty in the fairy tale was awakened by the kiss of her prince. Finley woke up to the overwhelming and oh-so-not-delightful smell of vinegar.

"Bloody hell!" she cried, lurching upright. Her voice sounded like the scratch of metal on cobblestone and her throat was tender to the touch. Would it bruise in the form of handprints?

Griffin sat beside her. They were on the settee. Someone had elevated her feet and removed her boots and, from the feel of it, loosened her corset. Under ordinary circumstances the realization that she was partially disrobed on a sofa with Griffin would lead to heart palpitations, but not now. Not when he was looking at her as though her being attacked by a dead person was his fault.

Because she had the sinking feeling that it probably was.

Sam and Jasper lurked nearby. Sam held a small blue glass bottle and a handkerchief. He'd been the one to administer the foul-smelling restorative. No doubt he'd asked for the privilege to wake her so rudely.

At least there was no sign of Mei. Other than a broken vase on the floor, wet carpet and trampled flowers, there was no indication that Finley had almost... well, given up the ghost.

"What was that?" she demanded hoarsely.

"It was Mei," Griffin replied—rather unnecessarily.

"I know that. *Why* was it Mei?"

"Yeah," Jasper joined in. "I reckon you've got some explainin' to do, Griff." The cowboy did not look happy, and why would he? He'd loved Mei once, been betrayed by her and then held her as she died. If anyone deserved answers, it was him.

Griffin rose from the settee and walked a few feet away, then he turned to face the three of them. He looked annoyed, frightened and somewhat relieved. It was obvious he didn't want to tell them, but also that he knew he had no other choice.

"I'm being haunted."

They stared at him.

"Haunted?" Finley echoed, coming up on her elbows. "By Mei?"

He ran a hand through his hair. "By someone, though it's obvious Mei is part of it."

"Just part?" Sam asked. "Good Lord, man how many ghosts do you have chasing your tail?"

"Mei's the only one who I see clearly. The rest are black wisps—like shadows."

Sam again. "So this started in New York."

Griffin nodded. "In Tesla's apartments. At first I thought it was something strange within the Aether, but after we returned to England I realized that Mei had returned with us. The wisps, too. I'm not sure why it's happening or how to stop it. That's why I asked for Isley's assistance." He glanced at Finley. "Mei won't speak to me. She only attacks and screams silently at me. I hoped he could ascertain just what it is she wants, or find a way to give her peace."

"I don't reckon peace is something she ever courted," Jasper lamented.

Finley ignored him. Mei had played Jasper for a fool and tried to get her killed. She didn't care if the witch suffered eternal torment. There were more important things to address right now.

"This has been going on for weeks and you never

told us?" She couldn't keep the disbelief, or the disappointment, from her voice. "I would have liked to have been prepared for the possibility that a ghost might try to strangle me to death!"

"Just how did she manage that, anyway?" Sam asked. "I thought it was rare for ghosts to interact with regular people."

Regular people? There was nothing *regular* about any of them.

"It is," Griffin said with a slight sigh. "It's as though she's siphoning strength from somewhere. Isley believes she might be using my own affinity with the Aether against me."

That was bloody brilliant. Just wonderful.

"You should have told us," she admonished him. "You didn't need to go through this alone." And that was the real issue. It wasn't that she thought he didn't trust her—it was the fact that he thought dealing with this was something he needed to do by himself.

"I thought I was the only one in danger." Griffin confessed as he massaged the back of his neck. He looked like hell, but she wasn't going to hand over her sympathy quite so easily. "Fin, if I thought for a moment she'd try to hurt you..."

"She didn't just try, Griffin. She almost choked the life out of me."

"I didn't want you all to get involved," he confided. "I knew you'd try to help and I was afraid you would get hurt."

She actually smiled. He was such a martyr at times. "That worked out well, didn't it?"

He returned the grin. He looked as though the weight of the world had been lifted off his shoulders. "Rather brilliantly, I thought."

"Right, so the two of you have kissed and made up," Sam butted in. "Then maybe you could help me figure out how to bring Emily home. We can deal with Griffin's ghost after that."

He was right, of course. She was upset that Griffin hadn't shared with her what he was going through, but she also understood that he didn't want to involve them for fear they'd be hurt. Only now, she was involved whether either of them liked it or not.

Sam turned to Jasper. "I mean no disrespect to Mei's memory, Renn, but my priority is finding Emily and keeping her alive."

The American shrugged. "I'm with ya, my friend." He looked at Griffin. His golden-green eyes were troubled. "The Mei I knew wouldn't torment anyone like that."

Griffin nodded, expression grim. "She's angry, and I don't blame her."

"Huh." Jasper shook his head. "I do."

Finley couldn't contain her surprise. Since coming back to London, Jasper hadn't said much of anything about what happened in New York and said even less to Griffin. Maybe his move to King House should've been proof enough that he held no ill will toward them.

Griffin looked as though he didn't know whether to laugh or cry. He merely smiled a tight, stretched smile. "I blame myself."

"Did you know she'd get trapped in the wall?" Jasper asked.

"Of course not!"

"Then there's no blame for you to take. I shouldn't have left her with Dalton. I shouldn't have done a lot of things, but none of them make a lick of difference now."

"No, they don't," Sam interjected. "Mei's dead and she's pissed, I get it. But if you don't mind, I'd like to talk about Emily, who is still alive and doesn't blame anyone for anything. I'd really like to find her if you're all done with your own little dramas."

That put them all in their places, didn't it? Thoroughly chastised, Finley replied, "You said we couldn't go charging in because the machines might detect us. But would they detect another machine?"

Griffin shot her a glance that made even her toes shiver. He might be a maddening, frustrating, stubborn bit of bone, but he was so very, very fine. "What do you have in mind?" he asked.

Oh, she had a list. But he was talking about rescuing Emily, so she put her mind to that instead. "Well, surely Emily has some automaton or device we can send into the catacombs to spy for us."

"The cat?" Griffin asked, looking to Sam.

The big lad looked surprised to be consulted. He was normally called upon for his strength, not his wits. Finley pushed that thought away. That was unfair. She'd hate to be treated as though she hadn't much intelligence just because she was strong.

"Not the cat," he said. "It's too big and too flashy. It'll be noticed, nabbed and probably stripped for parts or, worse, turned against us."

"Emily would never forgive us if it was destroyed," Finley added.

Sam nodded. "Exactly. She's got some smaller automatons in the lab. I'll check and see if there's anything we can use."

"I might be able to alter the device's Aetheric frequency," Griffin threw in. "It would make something small all that more difficult to detect."

"I'll go down there now and see what I can find."

"I'm with you," Jasper said, casting a glance first at Finley and Griffin. "We'll leave the two of you to continue your conversation."

Finley's brows shot up. Griffin looked surprised, as well, and when the door closed, leaving them alone in the room, they turned to face each other awkwardly. "I'm sorry," he began. "I'm not used to explaining myself and even less accustomed to having anyone who cares."

"I care." And it didn't matter how embarrassing it was to admit it.

"Yes." He made the word longer than it ought to be. "Yes, you do. I'm not sure why. It's not as though I've been a charming, attentive suitor."

She tried not to smile—she should be angry with him, blast it. "Are you my suitor?"

"Do you have someone else in mind for the position?"

"No. But we live in the same house. There are some who might call you my protector." It was a joke. Sort of. Many rich men lived with or set up houses for ladies with whom they spent time but were not married to.

Griffin's jaw tightened. "Don't say that. Don't ever talk about yourself, or me, that way. I would never treat you like that."

"I know that. It was a stupid joke."

He looked like he didn't quite believe her. "Do you think I intentionally keep things from you to hurt you?"

In a rare moment of clarity, Finley stopped to consider her words. "I know you don't. I know you want to protect those you care about, and it drives you mad when you feel you've failed to do so. What you don't seem to realize is that you're mortal, and you need friends watching your back as much as the rest of us. Maybe even more."

His shoulders stiffened. "I was raised knowing that many people would depend on me for their safety and their livelihood. Regardless of what Jasper says, I am responsible for Mei's death. Nothing can change that."

"No, it can't, but rather than letting her punish you—and punishing yourself—maybe you should concentrate on giving that peace you mentioned. Make amends and stop flogging yourself. It's not terribly attractive."

To her surprise he laughed. "What would I do without you to give me clarity?"

"I imagine you'd suffocate yourself by shoving your head too far up your own backside."

He looked sheepish, but he was smiling, so he knew she was teasing. "I've never had to answer to anyone. I've never really had anyone else I can depend upon other than Sam. As duke it's my job to take care of others, not to let them take care of me. I'll try, though, for you."

Oh. That was exactly the right thing to say. It thrilled and scared her at the same time.

But there was more. "I can't promise that I'll never be an ass, or that I'll never make you cry. I can't promise that I won't make you so angry you want to cosh me over the head with a brick. I can't promise you forever, Finley. I'd love to, but I can give you right now. I can give you me in all my defective glory."

She looked up at him, eyes burning with tears she refused to shed. "Don't you ever shut up?" she demanded.

And then tossing frustration and vexation to the wind, she threw her arms around his neck and kissed him.

That was the end of any and all conversation.

Chapter 10

Leonardo Garibaldi was fragile, vulnerable. He was no threat to her safety whatsoever, and would be incredibly easy to kill *if* Emily could just get close enough to do it without a bloody piece of metal watching her.

She hadn't lost her nerve, nor did she think she would be able to do the deed without it changing her forever. Anyone who could kill and not feel the gravity of it was probably not right in the head. It was why opposite sides in a war were made to think of each other as enemies that would kill them if they didn't shoot first. They were taught to think of each other as evil, because no sane man or woman could walk up to another and put a bullet in their belly without the justification of doing it to protect themselves, their loved ones, their country, or their cause.

Emily looked at it as preventing someone truly evil from walking the earth, but more importantly, she would do it to protect her friends. She would do it for Sam, and she would gladly bear the weight of her actions. She would bear it without regret, and that was as disturbing as it was comforting.

She didn't court death, nor was she happy about having to take a life, but it was Garibaldi, and if ever there was a man who needed killing, it was him. She could accept the responsibility that came with it, she could almost convince herself that it was something she would happily die to accomplish. That was a lie, of course. She didn't want to die. Didn't want to die without seeing Sam one last time.

But, this was the man responsible for the machine that killed Sam. If she got the chance, she would make certain Garibaldi never hurt anyone again.

She stood in front of the tank, staring at the Machinist's broken body as it floated in the viscous fluid. The wounds and bones had healed, but the machines that put him in this...soup didn't have much more than a working knowledge of the human form and how it reacted to organite. She supposed that the automatons believed putting him in the tank would be enough to heal him, but they hadn't set his bones or assessed internal damage.

He would make a fortune for a freak show were he to be exhibited. Perhaps one would purchase his corpse once his brain was removed from it.

"Victoria" checked the oxygenation levels of the fluid and the input/output stations. The machines "fed" their master through a tube that traveled from a cask of mush into the tank, into his mouth and down into his stomach. Waste material was collected by other tubes and disposed of in a small cauldron with a sealed lid to prevent stink. Sometimes she curled her nose at the smell when new waste flushed through the tubes, but for the most part it was easy to ignore, having grown up with an outdoor privy.

"I've been reading the material you gave me," she told it. It was easier to think of it as machine rather than a living thing because its organic composition was starting to break down. The organites had managed to keep the decay at a minimum, but eventually the old gal was going to rot away, leaving nothing behind but her internal metal workings and pieces of the glass eyes Garibaldi had given her that hadn't been taken over by living tissue.

"I've been reading the material you gave me, *ma'am,*" it corrected her. "We did not expect that you would not."

Was it part of the automaton's programming that made her believe she was some sort of monarch, or was it a side effect of the injury it had sustained and the slow decay that followed? Regardless, sometimes it reminded her of her great-grandmother, Brigit, who thought she was the queen of Ireland.

"You do realize that all of this may be futile, right? We very well might not succeed." In fact, it was almost certain that "they" wouldn't. She spoke as though they were coconspirators in the hope that she might eventually win over the insane bucket of flesh and bolts.

Its short, round frame groaned as it moved around the tank to check another valve. "We are aware of the lack of success. We are also confident that we will not fail."

"What makes you so certain?"

"We have you, and you have great motivation to see this endeavor to the end."

Motivation—a passive way of reminding her that her life was on the line. "There is no guarantee the organites will be able to engage and keep his brain operating."

"Endeavor 312's brain is almost fully formed. She possesses the Master's genetic biological material. His tissue will bond with hers, and return him to his flock once more."

"But you'll kill 312 in the meantime." It was still a ridiculous name. And it was ridiculous to expect that the brain of one being would automatically assimilate tissue from another's, no matter how much biological similarity they might share or how many organites you soaked them in.

Still, she wasn't going to argue about it, because right now that misconception was all that was keeping her alive.

"It was for this purpose that 312 was formed. It would have been preferable if the organic material had made her male, but that is of little consequence. She is well aware of the reason for her design and the honor that comes with it."

That was another point Emily wasn't about to argue, because arguing with machines never amounted to anything. This...*thing* talking to her might look vaguely human, but it wasn't, and it wasn't ever going to be, now. It had perhaps half a soul, if that, while 312 was well on her way to becoming the first organically man-ufactured human.

The scientific community would go mad to get their hands on her. For that matter, Emily herself would love to study 312's biological and mechanical construct. She was the first true example of *Deus ex machina*—God from the machine. The church would condemn her as a blasphemer, and say she had no soul, but 312 could reason and feel. Indeed, 312 was so close to human the line was practically nonexistent.

Emily would not take the brain out of a living person so that another could take its place. There was no contest. However, she could not allow 312 to run free in the world. She would be like a child who hadn't been told how to behave.

Odd, she was having more of a moral dilemma over 312 than Garibaldi.

"I'll need some of my equipment for the procedure."

"No."

It had been worth the attempt. She hadn't expected a yes. "Victoria" might be a machine, but she wasn't dumb. And there was no way she would be allowed to return to King House, unless she had some magic device that might allow her to perform brain surgery.

"Fine, but I'm going to need some supplies."

"We will procure whatever is deemed necessary."

Emily cocked her chin. What was this monstrosity's idea of "necessary"? "I'll make a list."

"We will insure paper and a pencil is brought to your cell. You may return there now."

For all this talk of her being the "mother" she was treated more like a prisoner. Common sense suggested that she was perhaps both. The machines thought she was something special and they needed her, so they'd do whatever they could to make certain she didn't get away.

As she turned to return to her cell she glanced over her shoulder and saw "Victoria" take one of the cables from the tank and insert the end of it into her mouth. Bubbles rose to the surface of the tank. Were Garibaldi's eyelids twitching?

They were communicating. Garibaldi and his creation had formed some sort of symbiotic relationship. Did the Machinist have an ability similar to Emily's own that allowed him to understand the language of metal?

Did he know she was there? Was he afraid? He should be.

That list of items she needed was going to include a few things that would enable her to contact Griffin. Or Sam. She might be able to send a signal that Sam's automatonical parts would "hear." Would he know what to do with it was the question.

Emily walked into the room that was her home for now to find 312 sitting on her bed. The frame sagged under the weight of her skeleton. The metal inside her was lightweight, but still more dense than bone.

"What are you doing in here?"

The girl stood. She looked even more human than she had earlier. The organites were working at an incredible rate inside her. Within a few days it would be almost impossible to tell that she hadn't been born human. It would be completely impossible once she learned the nuances of human behavior.

"I thought you might like something to read." She gestured to several piles of books in the corner. "I didn't know what you would like, so I brought them all."

Emily arched a brow. There were a lot of books there—many more than there had been when she first woke up. "Thank you." Then, as the thought occurred to her, "Can you read?"

She shook her head. "Not well. I know some words, but not enough. I would love to be able to read." This was said with such wistfulness that Emily smiled. She had no business feeling anything for this creature, least of all kindness.

At least Garibaldi hadn't forgotten to make word

recognition part of her programming. "Pick one that you like the look of," she suggested. "I'll teach you."

A bright smile lit the girl's face. Her teeth were almost fully formed. Only a scant few were shorter than they ought to be. "That would be lovely. Thank you!"

Emily sat down on the narrow bed and waited for 312 to return. The book she brought with her was an illustrated version of *The Adventures of Pinocchio* by Carlo Collodi.

"This is an interesting choice," Emily remarked, trying to sound casual, even though her heart had somersaulted in her chest. "Why did you pick it?"

The girl shrugged. "It looks nice. And I think…I think the puppet boy in the pictures is like me."

Emily bit the inside of her lip to keep tears from filling her eyes. She cleared her throat. "He wants to be a real boy."

Wide eyes met hers. "Does he get his wish?"

"We'll have to read the book to find out. Open it to the first page and we'll begin."

Smiling happily, 312 opened the book with long, nimble fingers. She had hands like Jasper's, only more feminine. "I thought of a name I like."

"Oh? What?"

"Emelia. It's like your name, but different."

Emily's throat tightened. This was so confusing. She didn't want to like this creature, but she was as endearing as anyone could possibly be. "It's a good name. I think it would be even better if we thought of a name that would be just yours."

She thought for a moment. "Maybe Mila? I like the sound of that."

"Mila." Emily gave a nod of approval. "That's a fine name. It suits you." And it was further proof that she was becoming human; she was developing a sense of individuality—a sense of self.

"I'll tell the others not to call me 312 anymore. I'll be Mila from now on."

Emily forced a smile. The machines would not understand her need for a name. "Victoria" especially would not be pleased. If 3...*Mila* began thinking of herself as a person and not the vessel for the Machinist, things would not go well. What would happen if she asserted herself as an individual? What would they do to her? What would they make Emily do to her?

And even more frightening—what would Mila do in return?

When Sam and Jasper found them later, Finley and Griffin had stopped kissing and...other things that made her face hot when she thought about them. Their clothing was a little rumpled, but neither of the boys seemed to notice, or if they did they wisely said nothing.

Finley's stomach was a butterfly cage, flitting and twitching like a thousand wings fluttered inside it. They hadn't done anything too improper, but her experience with blokes wasn't terribly extensive, unless she counted the ones she'd thrashed for being impertinent. Regardless, what she and Griffin had done left her giddy, curious and in want of more.

Of course, as soon as she looked at Sam, guilt washed over her. Emily—one of her dearest friends—was missing and she'd spent the previous fifteen minutes with her hands under Griffin's shirt while Sam searched for a way to find the little redhead who meant so much to him.

"Did you find something?" she asked him, running a hand over the tangled mess of her hair. Her corset was slightly askew as well, the front busk about an inch to the right of center—just enough to feel odd.

"I think so." From his waistcoat pocket he withdrew something made of brass that was approximately the same circumference as a silver dollar and set it upon the desktop.

It was a mechanical spider, its thin legs reticulated

and delicately detailed. Even its round little backside was etched with a scrolling pattern.

"How pretty," Finley remarked. She wasn't a big fan of spiders in general, but this one looked as though it could be a piece of jewelry. "What does it do?"

"I think it acts like a homing pigeon."

"You think?" she teased.

His cheeks turned pink. "I remember Emily telling me about it. It's like a tracker, but it's tuned to Emily's Aetheric signature. She was going to attune it to all of us, but she only got as far as herself."

Griffin picked the small spider up and studied it. "So, if we put this thing in the catacombs below Saint Pancras, it will lead us to Emily."

Sam nodded. "It should."

Peering over Griffin's shoulder, Finley thought the machine was as good an idea as any. "Will other machines be able to detect it?"

"I don't think so." Despite his words, his voice was confident. "There are so many automatons in the underground every day that detecting a new signal, especially one I dampen, would be difficult if not impossible. Meanwhile, it should transmit back to us Emily's exact location."

Should was a tricky word, wasn't it? "How do we track it?"

Sam held up a small compass. "Once the device is put to work, it will send a signal to the compass, which will lead us to Emily's location. It vibrates when the target is nearby."

It wasn't perfect, but it was the best thing they had other than the cat, which would be discovered for certain.

"Do it," Griffin said, giving the spider to Sam. "If it can find Em it's worth the risk."

His large head nodded, closing his fingers around the little machine. "I'll take it to a spot not far from Saint Pancras and let it go."

"Just go into the station," Jasper suggested. "Won't that be closer?"

"We don't know what we're up against," Sam reminded him. "I'm going to assume that whoever has Em knows all about the rest of us. I'd rather not let them know we're coming for them. If that's all right by you."

It took Finley a moment to realize Sam was speaking specifically to Griffin rather than the three of them. Sam's father had worked for Griffin's, who had taken him in when Sam began to show signs of the same heightened evolution as his own son. The two of them had grown up together, but it was obvious that as good of friends as they were, Sam deferred to Griffin because that was what lower class people did.

"Of course it is," Griffin responded. "I trust your judgment, Sam. We'll do whatever you think best on this one. I just want to bring Em home."

If Griffin had given Sam a puppy she didn't think the fellow could look any more pleased. Realization knocked hard against her thick skull. If Griffin was going to try to not be the Duke of Greythorne all the time and go all lord of the manor on them, then they owed it to him and themselves not to act like he was their superior. They were a unit, not a dukedom.

While Sam was out releasing the tracking spider, Finley, Griffin and Jasper began combing through the daily papers for strange crimes or occurrences. A blank-faced automaton man and Queen Victoria could not just be running amok beneath the city without some notice. No ransom demands for Emily's return had been received, so they went on the assumption that the machines wanted her for something.

"Here's mention of a robbery in Covent Garden," Finley piped up, scanning the text. "Says that a group of workmen who were painting a theater had some of their equipment stolen—pulleys and rope."

Griffin glanced up. "That might be what we're looking for, or it could be completely random. Set it aside
just in case."

"I might have something," Jasper joined in, giving
the paper a snap so it was stiff in his hands. "A scientific medical society who had a large fish tank stolen
from their premises a couple of months ago just re-
ported another robbery. Looks like some scoundrels
made off with quite a bit of surgical equipment and
biological matter."

Griffin and Finley exchanged a look. "Biological
matter?" they chorused.

"That could be anything," Griffin continued, "but
when it's stolen along with surgical equipment that
means that someone needs medical attention."

Jasper was still reading. "Goes on to say that wit-
nesses saw a 'strange' machine that resembled a large
spider near the building, and that it appeared to have a
crate on its back."

"A crate could carry a lot of equipment and biological matter," Finley remarked.

Griffin frowned. "Automaton crimes. That sounds
like Garibaldi's usual sort of behavior. The biological
matter is what bothers me."

"Why?" Finley asked.

"Years ago, before my parents were killed, a friend of my father's suffered an awful injury. He was very badly burned and no one expected him to live, and if he did he would be seen as a monster for the rest of his life. My father filled an old copper tub with a vile concoction of organic material—plant and animal, along with organites—immersed the man in the tub, ran a breathing tube into his mouth and then sat back and waited."

"Did he survive?"

Griffin ran a hand through his thick hair. "Not only that, but he was completely healed. Not even the tiniest scar."

"So, if the thefts are connected, the automatons could be healing someone?" Her immediate thought was Garibaldi. He had to be the first person Griffin thought of as well, judging from the expression on his face.

"I don't want to jump to any wild conclusions just yet," he said. "The thefts might not even be connected. The automatons might have another use for those particular items."

Jasper set the paper aside. "Might not want to jump to conclusions, but it don't hurt to prepare for any eventuality. I don't much like thinking of Mei as a vengeful spirit, but I can't deny what I saw." His gaze locked with Griffin's. "You don't deserve to be punished for what you did. I know you'd take it back if you could."

Griffin inclined his head. "In a heartbeat."

Finley kept her mouth shut. Mei would have cheerfully slit her throat, and let Jasper take the blame for a murder she committed. Her death was unfortunate, but Finley preferred that outcome to her own death— and those of her friends. Mei made her own dark side seem sweet and innocent. Almost.

"Jas," Griffin went on a second later. "Could you… would you, mind sitting in on my next session with Isley? Mei may be calmer if she comes and sees you."

"I'll do what I can. Not sure how much help I'll be."

"I hope that she might talk to you. Would you be agreeable with that?"

"I would," Jasper said after a pause. "If it helps her move on, and stops her from attacking my friends, I'll talk to her."

Yes, wouldn't want to keep Mei from her appointment with the devil. Oh, she was so judgmental, but really, if you couldn't wish hell on those who tried to kill you and your friends, who could you wish it on?

As soon as the thought crossed her mind, Finley felt a breath of icy air on the back of her neck. Every hair stood straight on end. *Brilliant.*

"I have a feeling the two of you won't have to wait long." The words had barely left her mouth when she caught the faintest glimpse of the ghost. Maybe she could see her now because she had once before, or perhaps Mei was getting stronger, because Jasper appeared to see her, also. To Griffin she would appear almost as solid as anything in this world.

Black, wispy tendrils floated around her, like seaweed in the ocean. They were with her, but not of her. These were the things that had attacked Griffin in New York. What were they doing with Mei? Had they brought her, or had she brought them?

"Mei?" Poor Jasper looked like hell. His face was white, his eyes huge. The ghost looked at Jasper for a moment, expression sad, before turning on Finley.

She didn't look so sad now! In fact, she looked angry. Frustrated. She opened her mouth to speak, but no sound came out.

"What do you want?" Griffin asked, his voice strong and commanding.

The wisps broke away from Mei and launched themselves at him, turning into teeth and claws. One raked his face and drew blood. The others converged. Griffin made a strangled grunt of pain.

They would rip him apart.

"Stop it," Finley commanded, clenching her fists as she took a step closer to Mei. "Make them stop."

The ghost looked at her and shook her head, holding up her hands in supplication. Frustration mounted in Finley's gut. Was Mei trying to tell her that she couldn't stop them, or was she just being a bitch?

She tried again. "Stop them."

Mei shook her almost translucent head, and then pointed at Finley. No need to guess what she meant by that.

"How am I supposed to do it?" If Griffin couldn't and his power was the Aether, how the devil could she have any effect on them?

Mei held out her hands, as though she was about to wrap them around Finley's throat.

"Finley, don't." Jasper shot her a fearful glance.

Finley turned her head. Griffin was still on his feet as he battled the wisps, but his face had been clawed on both sides and his neck was bleeding. She could either trust Mei or let those tendrils of black have him.

"You better not be lying to me," she warned Mei. "If I die, I'm going to kick your arse, understood?"

Mei nodded.

"Do it, then."

"Finley, no!" Jasper reached out for her, lightning

quick, but his former love had no substance on this plane, not unless she wanted to.

The hands that closed around her throat were bone-chillingly cold and so very strong. They cut off Finley's air immediately, leaving her gasping and choking. She looked into those black eyes and saw nothing. Mei's mouth was grim, and there was no joy in her expression. She was killing Finley, but she wasn't enjoying it.

Blackness swamped the perimeter of her mind, darkening her vision. Blood roared in her ears as she slowly sank into oblivion. Mei kept squeezing. Finley forced herself not to struggle, not to fight. She heard Griffin shout her name.

And then she died.

Chapter 11

The world of the dead was not what Finley expected.

She expected something out of one of Mr. Dickens's stories—all torment and rattling chains. Instead, she found herself in a world washed with a blue-gray tinge that reminded her of Griffin's eyes, and it felt a peaceful place.

Now she knew why people referred to it as "beyond the veil." It did have a diaphanous sort of quality to it, like it was trapped in gauze placed over the living world. It gently tugged at her soul, filling her with that peace, that sense of rest.

She could stay here forever. No one would judge

here. No one would ever make her wonder if they cared about her or not. She'd never have to explain herself....

A sharp pain in her ribs snapped her out of the languid feeling taking over her body. But it wasn't really her body, was it? Because her body was two feet away, and Mei was standing next to her with her arms folded over her chest. She had bony elbows for a ghost. Finley rubbed her side.

"All right, you've killed me. Now what?" she demanded. Perhaps she ought to be a bit more upset about being dead, but she couldn't quite manage it. She felt as though she was about to set forth on a wondrous journey....

"Ow! Bloody hell, stop jabbing me! What?"

Mei pointed. "Look, you stupid girl!"

Finley followed her finger, ignoring the insult. There was Griffin, and he was being attacked by angry wisps of black that seemed to have teeth and claws though they had no real form.

Viciously, she turned on Mei. "Are you doing that?" What was she going to do if she was? Stare her to death? Mei could touch her but... Wait. This was the Aether. Right now she was technically dead.

"No," Mei retorted. "But I can't touch them, and he can't hear me."

Finley threw herself at Griffin's attackers. If she was dead, she didn't have much time before she stayed that way, maybe Griffin, too.

Her hands stung as she seized one of the wisps. Blood welled up around the black, trickling down her wrist. Little buggers hurt.

Griffin's face was bloody, his neck and hands, too. His body glowed with his power, but the wisps didn't seem to care; in fact, they seemed to feed on it. The more he fought the more delicious they found him.

Bloody little demons. "Griffin, stop struggling!"

He didn't hear her. His power was building, the light around him increasing its halo. It brightened, pulsed…

"Oh, bugger." Finley threw her arms up in front of her face just in time. The light coming off Griffin exploded into a kaleidoscope of color, raining down tiny iridescent snowflakes that were hot to the touch.

The wisps backed off. There were fewer of them now. Finley watched in horror as they grew in size, claws and fangs elongating. The blast had only made them stronger. They drew themselves up, preparing to attack.

Right. That was enough of that nonsense. She didn't care what they did to her, but they would not take Griffin.

She stepped in front of him and smiled gently at his ravaged face.

"Fin," he whispered, eyes widening. "Don't."

"I've got this," she promised. "I need you to bring me back, Griffin. Don't let me die, all right?"

He nodded. It was the oddest thing, because in the Aether he retained the same form he had in the mortal realm. Finley watched him through the veil as he moved to where her body sprawled on the floor.

"You just going to stand there?" she asked Mei.

The girl shrugged. "I told you I cannot touch them. Whatever keeps me here also keeps me from interfering. Now stop talking and fight."

She was right, of course, though Finley bristled at the words. The wisps, done with waiting, surged after Griffin, but Finley stepped into their path. Drawing back her fist, she sent it forward as if her muscles were coiled springs. Her knuckles connected with the wisp as hard as she could punch.

It was like hitting a brick wall. They might look as insubstantial as clouds, but the little demons were much, much more, which was a good thing in this case. The one she hit flew backward and broke apart, evaporating into nothing.

Another came at her and she hit it, as well. Then another, and another…

"Finley."

Another.

"Finley."

Only two more left…now one.

"Finley!" She glanced over her shoulder. It was Griffin. He was poised above her body, pushing on her chest. In the Aether, she could feel his hands pulling at her. Whatever he was doing, it was something to force her into her body. It was to save her life.

She turned her attention back to the last of the demons. It was bigger than the rest, and as she prepared to ram her bruised and bloodied knuckles into it, the swirling darkness took shape, morphing into a face.

The Machinist.

Finley's lips curled into a sneer. "I'm going to enjoy smashing you to bits."

The coal-dust mouth opened. "Not today, my dear," it rumbled. And then, before she could even react, Garibaldi's shadowy self launched itself at Mei. He caught her in monstrous claws that sprang from hands that hadn't been there two seconds ago. She screamed and was swallowed into the darkness as it collapsed on itself, disappearing completely.

Finley could only stare after it.

"Finley!" It was Griffin again. This time, there was real fear in his voice. At first she'd thought about staying in this place, but she couldn't—not with him waiting for her on the other side. She had no idea how to get back into her body, but she knew she had to figure it out and fast, or the decision to stay or leave would be made for her.

"Griffin." She stared at him helplessly.

For a split second terror sparked in his eyes. He held out his hand; his fingers pierced the veil as they reached for her. Finley entwined her fingers with his, relief washing over her. He was as real in this world as he was in the living. Of course he was.

Their gazes locked. She trusted that his abilities could take her back to the world of the living. She smiled as he pulled her closer to her body. Her vision blurred as she passed through the mist, fading to serene darkness....

She lurched upright with a strangled gasp, back arching as breath forced itself into her lungs. Coming alive wasn't nearly as pleasant as dying had been.

"It's all right," a soothing voice said near her ear. "You're safe."

Gasping, but breathing, she turned her head. Griffin's face was just inches from hers. He was bloody, but gorgeous all the same. His fingers were still wrapped around hers, warm and strong. He held her hand as though he'd never let it go. She could lean into him, let him put his arms around her. She wanted to press her mouth against his and not stop until they both suffocated. She wanted to take him to the carpet and...

"Fin?"

She lifted her gaze. Griffin's was bright and focused so exactly on her that she knew he harbored similar thoughts. His fingers tightened around hers. She felt herself tilting toward him, as he moved toward her.

"Ahem."

Finley started. Damnation, she'd forgotten about Jasper. Slowly, she and Griffin turned their flushed faces toward their friend. He looked anxious.

"What the devil just happened?" he demanded. "After Mei faded, all I saw was Finley pass out and then Griffin's face was getting cut up."

Griffin withdrew a handkerchief from his pocket and began wiping the blood from his face. His coat was shredded but seemed to have protected him from the worst of the attack. "It was Mei," he said. "Mei and Garibaldi."

Jasper paled.

"Mei was trying to help," Finley told him. "If not for

her I wouldn't have been able to get into the Aether to assist Griffin. She couldn't do it." She glanced at Griffin. "She said she was being controlled—by Garibaldi. He seems to control the wisps, as well."

"Wisps?" Jasper asked. "Like what you saw at Tesla's?"

Griffin nodded, grimacing at the amount of blood on the square of white linen in his hands. "I've come to think of them as Aether demons. They are malevolent by nature."

Jasper snorted. "You don't say. Why could Finley see them and not me?"

"That I don't know." He tossed the bloody cloth onto a small table. "They seem to be able to conceal or reveal themselves at will."

"Garibaldi's will," Finley corrected. "I saw his face. He spoke. And he took Mei."

Jasper's jaw flexed. "The bastard's controlling her."

Finley opened her mouth and closed it so fast her teeth clacked together. It wasn't her place to point out to Jasper that Mei had betrayed him and that he shouldn't make her a victim just because she apologized before she died. Saying she was sorry didn't change anything.

Finley was sorry that she had kicked Sam in the chest so hard she'd almost killed him, but that didn't change the fact that she'd done it, and that she'd done it on purpose. She hadn't given any thought to how badly she might injure him. All she cared about was defending herself against his assault because he had seemed ready to kill her.

Mei hadn't cared who she hurt, either.

"Seems to me if we find Garibaldi and end him for certain, all of our problems will disappear—including Mei's servitude to the bastard." The cowboy looked at the two of them as though he thought they might argue. "We'll destroy his metal and bring Emily home."

"As soon as we have an idea of where she is, we will go and bring her home." Griffin's expression hardened. "I will take care of Garibaldi, and this time I'll make certain he doesn't come back."

Finley's heart skipped a beat. He was very impressive when he was out for blood. Speaking of which…

"Come on," she said, taking him by the hand. "Let's get those cuts attended to. I'm not as experienced a doctor as Em, but I reckon I can do a good enough job."

He smiled at her—a subtle lopsided tilt of his mouth that filled her stomach with the fluttering wings of a thousand butterflies. His thumb brushed the back of her battered knuckles.

She swallowed. A fellow shouldn't be allowed to make a girl feel so…vulnerable. He patted Jasper on the shoulder as they walked past. "I'll make sure she gets peace, Jas. I promise."

Jasper seemed to realize that Griffin needed to do this as much for himself as for Jasper, or even Mei. He needed to atone, whether or not it was necessary.

Griffin might need to make amends, but it was Finley's job to make sure Garibaldi didn't kill him before he got the chance. His life was in her hands, and she was going to keep a very, *very* tight grip on it.

Mila's capacity for learning was amazing and frightening at the same time. Emily hypothesized that a very small part of the girl's brain still functioned as a logic engine, absorbing and processing information at a remarkable rate.

This was their second reading lesson, if it could be called such. Every once in a while Mila would stumble over a word, or inquire as to its meaning. She'd been programmed for language, so once her internal workings began to understand the data being taken in, it wasn't long before she began to work out meaning, pronunciation and application.

She was going to be a highly intelligent person; that much was clear.

Emily lay on the cot with her eyes closed, listening

to the girl read. It wasn't as though she had anything else to do. She'd given that awful Victoria automaton her list of supplies and was waiting for them to arrive. Short of looking for something to poke a hole in the Machinist's tank, she didn't know what else she could accomplish. And it wasn't as though she could "do" anything when Mila was not only watching but practically locked in the room with her.

That was wrong. There was something she could do. Something she should have thought of before this. Obviously she wasn't as smart as she liked to think!

"I'm going to miss listening to you read."

Mila stopped reading and raised her head. It was probably just imagination at this point, but Emily fancied she could hear gears grinding. "Are you going away?"

"I'm hoping to eventually go home, but you'll be gone before me."

The girl frowned. The expression must have been new to her because her brow immediately relaxed, then furrowed again. She touched her fingers to her forehead, feeling the ridges. "Where am I going?"

Was it possible she didn't know? "I shouldn't have said anything. Pretend I didn't." Emily held her breath and waited.

The frown deepened. "I cannot pretend—that would be a lie. Tell me."

She might look like a normal girl—almost—but the important thing Emily had to remember was that Mila was still very much a machine in a few very pivotal ways. Or perhaps the better way to describe it was that she had a childlike naïveté about her. Having no wish to be on the receiving end of the sort of violence her incredibly strong limbs were capable of inflicting, Emily released her breath and hoped telling the truth didn't come back to slap her in the face.

"You know that you are to be the vessel for the Master." Calling Garibaldi by such a lofty title made her want to vomit.

"Yes. Her Majesty tells me it's a great honor."

Of course, the decaying, twisted form of flesh and metal would say that. "I reckon it is, but you won't be the same once that happens."

Mila's held tilted like an inquisitive puppy's. "I won't look the same?"

"You won't be the same. You will no longer exist." Oh, dear, perhaps this hadn't been such a brilliant idea.

The girl fell silent for a moment. "In the book, Pinocchio's nose grows whenever he tells a lie."

"Yes." This was a rather radical change of subject.

"Your nose hasn't grown at all."

Emily couldn't help but smile. "My nose doesn't grow when I tell a lie. Only Pinocchio's does that."

"Then how do I know you're not lying? Her Majesty told me you might lie to me. She said I oughtn't trust you." And then, "What is trust? I know the definition of the word, but not the emotion."

Yes, what a wonderful kettle of fish she'd jumped into! Emily sighed. "Right. When I tell you something, such as you are very pretty, do you believe me?"

"I don't know. Am I pretty?"

"Yes, you are. Very much so."

Mila preened. "Thank you."

"That's trust."

Skepticism glinted in her eyes—both now fully framed by long, thick lashes. "Telling me I'm pretty?"

"No. You believing me when I tell you that."

"I have no reason not to believe you."

"That means you trust me—at least to an extent." She was good at this teaching business!

Mila pondered this for a moment. What Emily would give to study how much of that process was actual brain activity versus logic engine computation! "Then trust is believing what someone tells you without any reason other than want."

"Sort of. I trust you not to hurt me. You trusted me to help you learn to read."

The girl nodded slowly. "I do not hurt you because I don't want to. I feel you are no threat to me. I think...I think I care for you. At least somewhat."

"Oh. Thank you. I like you, as well." And she did, even though it was probably a very bad idea. She rather felt like an older sister, and since she herself had only brothers, and was the youngest, she liked the unfamiliar feeling.

I can't let them put his brain in her. I can't let them ruin her. Emily knew her past played a large part in this sudden need to protect. Mila was sweet and innocent, and she was going to be used in a horrible fashion and then tossed away.

She knew what that felt like, to be used and tossed away like a broken doll.

But could she allow Mila to continue to evolve? To exist? If she did, the girl would be her responsibility, possibly for the rest of her life.

That just might be something she could live with.

"If the Master's brain is put in my head then he will become me?"

Emily nodded. "His consciousness will live inside

The frown deepened. "I cannot pretend—that would be a lie. Tell me."

She might look like a normal girl—almost—but the important thing Emily had to remember was that Mila was still very much a machine in a few very pivotal ways. Or perhaps the better way to describe it was that she had a childlike naïveté about her. Having no wish to be on the receiving end of the sort of violence her incredibly strong limbs were capable of inflicting, Emily released her breath and hoped telling the truth didn't come back to slap her in the face.

"You know that you are to be the vessel for the Master." Calling Garibaldi by such a lofty title made her want to vomit.

"Yes. Her Majesty tells me it's a great honor."

Of course, the decaying, twisted form of flesh and metal would say that. "I reckon it is, but you won't be the same once that happens."

Mila's held tilted like an inquisitive puppy's. "I won't look the same?"

"You won't be the same. You will no longer exist." Oh, dear, perhaps this hadn't been such a brilliant idea.

The girl fell silent for a moment. "In the book, Pinocchio's nose grows whenever he tells a lie."

"Yes." This was a rather radical change of subject.

"Your nose hasn't grown at all."

Emily couldn't help but smile. "My nose doesn't grow when I tell a lie. Only Pinocchio's does that."

"Then how do I know you're not lying? Her Majesty told me you might lie to me. She said I oughtn't trust you." And then, "What is trust? I know the definition of the word, but not the emotion."

Yes, what a wonderful kettle of fish she'd jumped into! Emily sighed. "Right. When I tell you something, such as you are very pretty, do you believe me?"

"I don't know. Am I pretty?"

"Yes, you are. Very much so."

Mila preened. "Thank you."

"That's trust."

Skepticism glinted in her eyes—both now fully framed by long, thick lashes. "Telling me I'm pretty?"

"No. You believing me when I tell you that."

"I have no reason not to believe you."

"That means you trust me—at least to an exte[nt]." She was good at this teaching business!

Mila pondered this for a moment. What Emily [would] give to study how much of that process was actua[lly] activity versus logic engine computation! "Th[en trust] is believing what someone tells you without [rea]son other than want."

your body, yes. His logic engine, if that makes it easier for you to understand."

"It does. I will look the same, but the way I process and assimilate information will be different." She paused. "I will no longer experience controlling my limbs or learning to read."

"Yes."

Wide eyes narrowed. "You look sad. When the transfer happens we will no longer be friends, will we?"

Emily shook her head, her throat tight. Lord, she was soft. Give her a lost kitten or stray automaton and she melted like warm butter. "No. Your master is my enemy."

This seemed to come as a surprise. "You don't want to put his brain in my head, do you?"

"I most certainly do not."

"If I understand the concept of life correctly, and the ways that humans can be destroyed, removing my brain will kill me. Death means you are gone forever, yes?"

Mary and Joseph, she was on the verge of tears. "Yes."

With the book still opened across her lap, Mila leaned forward, as though about to share a great secret. Her gaze remained fastened on Emily, who didn't care if the girl saw her wipe a spot of wet from her lashes.

"I think I trust you not to kill me, Emily."

Emily's eyes widened—yanked open by shock. "You do?"

"I think…I think you are my Geppetto. Are you not? Though, a mother rather than a father."

Oh, blast it all! Tears trickled down Emily's cheeks and she swiped at them with the back of her hand. She hadn't wanted to feel for this poor creature, and now here she was after a few days with her, bawling like a fool.

"You're leaking." Mila left her perch on a stack of books and came to kneel in front of the cot. She dabbed at Emily's cheeks with her sleeve. Poor thing obviously meant well, but Emily would be amazed if she didn't bruise from the force of the dabbing.

Emily sniffed. "I'm fine." And she was, until a pair of dangerously strong arms closed around her in a tentative and gentle grip. She found herself leaning into the embrace, her own arms going around Mila's back. She squeezed her eyes tight, fighting the tears until her head began to ache. Finally, the urge to cry eased and she opened her lids. She glanced up and saw a small, familiar shape on the ceiling. It was a mechanical spider.

It was *her* mechanical spider. Griffin must have sent it looking for her. It would transmit her exact location through the Aether back to King House. Her friends would come for her soon.

"I won't let them hurt you," she whispered, hugging the girl tight, and feeling only the softness of flesh rather than the unyielding strength of metal. "No one's ever going to hurt you."

And that promise extended not only to the Machinist and his "Victoria," but to the whole world. Anyone who tried to hurt this dear creature was going to be very, very sorry.

Chapter 12

"You don't have to look after me. I'm quite capable," Griffin protested as Finley cleaned the wounds on his face.

She paused from cleaning one particularly nasty cut along his left cheekbone. "Am I hurting you?" Lord, she had such a hard time meeting his gaze; she was afraid of what he might see in her eyes—the fear when she hadn't known how to help him, the sick feeling thinking that he might be seriously injured, the anger at him for playing martyr and keeping the "haunting" to himself for so long. Most of all, she was afraid he'd see that she was prepared to kill Garibaldi with her bare hands for him.

She'd do it and not even blink. That scared her. Not that she'd kill someone—she'd faced that prospect before—but that she'd do it for him without a thought.

"No," he murmured. "You're not hurting me. I'm afraid I've hurt you, though. Haven't I?"

She shrugged. "I'll get over it." That was true, but she still couldn't look him straight in the eye.

"I was only trying to protect you."

"I know that. I even appreciate it." Now she met his gaze. "I don't need to be protected."

The bounder actually smiled at her. "Sometimes you do. Sometimes I do, too." His smile faded. "Garibaldi and his demons have gotten stronger. They might have done severe damage to me had you not been there. Thank you."

Well, that sucked any residual anger out of her. "I don't want to be surprised like that again," she informed him. "If you're in trouble, you do what you expect the rest of us to do—share it so we can help."

"I'm not accustomed—"

"I know." She cut him off without remorse. "I don't care if you're the bloody Prince of bloody Wales. From now on you accept that you have friends who love you and stop trying to fix everything by yourself."

He actually looked surprised to be ordered about, but

he nodded. "You're right. I need to start playing by my
own rules, and stop being a hypocrite."

"It's not just that." She placed her palms gently on either side of his face so he couldn't look away. She took
care not to press on any of his wounds. "The rest of us
would be lost without you. We'd have no place to go,
no purpose. You've given us a home and made us feel
like heroes rather than freaks. You can't keep putting
yourself in danger when there are so many reasons for
you to live."

She released him, averting her gaze once more as she
took a jar of salve from the medical kit and removed
the top. It was Emily's special blend, made with organites. Each of them had enough of the "wee beasties" in
their system that healing took place rapidly, but some
injuries needed to disappear faster than others. People
would wonder what the Duke of Greythorne had done
to his handsome face. The salve would heal the shallow
wounds in a few hours, the deeper ones by morning.

Warm fingers brushed her cheek as she applied the
balm to his cleaned cuts. "Some reasons to live are more
dear than others."

Finley swallowed. Her heart kicked so hard against
her ribs she was certain it cracked a couple of them.
When she'd first met Griffin she'd believed him ca-

pable of mesmerism, and he did have some skill in that area, because even though she didn't want to look at him, her gaze betrayed her and met his.

Her heart stopped altogether. He was so...lovely. That was the only word that came to mind. His thumb traced the arch of her eyebrow, down to the curve of her cheekbone, and stroked. Then he placed his other hand on her face as well, holding her head as she had his just moments earlier. Now she was the one who couldn't look away.

"That night I found you I thought I could help you," he confessed.

"You did," she rasped. "You helped me combine the two sides of my nature."

"You're not done. You're still evolving into the woman you're meant to be. I worried that maybe my feelings for you would change once you integrated your dark half, that maybe that part of you would win dominance."

Finley's stomach turned. After all their kisses and embraces, was he going to tell her he didn't want her?

"Instead you've become even more amazing." His lips tilted lopsidedly as a glint lit his eyes. "I had no idea that you would change my life so much, that it had been so empty before you crashed into it. All that mattered was my duty and continuing my parents' work, continuing their service to the Crown. All of that still matters, but now you're the reason I want to make the world a better place. You're why I get up in the morning, simply because I cannot wait to see your face."

"That rhymes," she murmured inanely.

Griffin laughed. He brushed both thumbs over her cheeks. "The world's already a better place for having you in it, Finley Jayne."

She felt like Lizzie in *Pride and Prejudice* when Mr. Darcy reasserted his love for her. Her head spun as though she'd twirled around one too many times. "I don't know what to say."

"Then don't say anything."

They stared at each other for what felt like an eternity. He continued to look vaguely amused, while she was certain she looked like an idiot.

"It's a good thing I have an abundance of confidence," he joked. "Or I might take your silence for rejection."

Rejection? Good Lord, how could he even think such a thing? In fact, how could he be thinking of romance at all when the Machinist was still out there, still after him? "You're mad," she whispered. "We should be talking about what to do about Garibaldi, and how to keep you safe from his attacks. We should be talking about how to release his hold on Mei so she can move on."

"I know." One of his hands slid around to the back of her head. The other dropped to entwine with one of hers. He grinned like the madman he was. "But at the moment I really don't care."

And then he kissed her, and Finley didn't care about anything else, either.

Finley and Griffin were both asleep—fully clothed—when Sam barged into Griffin's bedroom sometime later. Still, Finley lurched upright, clutching at her shirt to make certain she was properly covered, cheeks flushing hot. Sam didn't seem to care one whit that she and Griffin were alone in his room, on his bed, but what if it had been Mrs. Dodsworth or one of the other servants? Or worse, Griffin's aunt Cordelia! It was scandalous behavior—the kind that could ruin her and give Griffin a bad reputation.

And then she remembered that none of that mattered, and that it wasn't Mrs. Dodsworth—who probably wouldn't say a word anyway—but it was Sam, who didn't care what she and Griffin did.

But *she* cared. The thought was somewhat surprising. What happened between herself and Griffin was no one's business.

"Don't you knock?" she demanded. "This is coming a bloody habit of yours."

Sam looked at her, and chose that precise moment to be a real human being rather than an aggravating half-wit. He actually blushed, which did nothing to ease her embarrassment. "Sorry. I think I found Emily."

She jumped off the bed and bounded over to him. "Where?"

He took a step back, like a large dog being approached by a small, yappy one. "Crestfield and Euston." He turned to Griffin, who had also risen. "Come downstairs, I'll show you on the map."

Sam preceded them out of the bedroom. Finley made to leave after him, but Griffin caught her by the hand and pulled her back.

"What?" she asked, noting the pensive expression on his healing face. The cuts left by Garibaldi's demons were little more than faint lines now.

"You haven't done anything wrong." Bloody hell, she hated it when he seemed to read her mind. "Sam's not going to judge you, or me."

"Maybe *I* judge me."

He arched a brow. "That's ridiculous." Finley's back

stiffened, but he went on, "You could have sneaked in here last night and ravished me and then skulked back to your own room without being seen and that would be fine, but get caught innocently sleeping and suddenly you're ruined."

Finley's lips twitched. "You reckon I'd ravage you, do you?"

He shrugged. "I'm surprised you've resisted temptation this long."

It was a cheeky remark, especially for him. It felt wrong, being lighthearted while Emily was missing, and probably in the hands of a madman, but this new intimacy between them had a giddiness to it that refused to be denied. She liked seeing him like this. For a moment she didn't think about the fact that the same lunatic that had Emily was also trying to kill Griffin. That was a sobering thought.

"Maybe I won't be able to resist much longer." Had she said that aloud? It was brazen, even for her, but with the danger surrounding them perhaps it was foolish to think that they had all the time in the world. Foolish to be afraid of sex when violence seemed to find her wherever she went.

His fingers tightened around hers. "I'm not going anywhere. Take your time."

Sometimes he knew exactly what to say, even when it contradicted her own thoughts. "Let's go see about bringing Emily home."

They walked downstairs together, still holding hands. For years the duality of Finley's nature had made her feel like she was an outsider to the rest of the world—in but not of. Not anymore. This was where she belonged. Griffin was who she belonged with. Their future was uncertain, but she planned on spending as much of it with him as time allowed.

And that was all the thought she was going to give it, because she was rapidly becoming sick of herself. She was a reasonably intelligent young woman who could take care of herself. She wasn't afraid of physical violence; in fact, part of her rather enjoyed it. Spending all this time fretting and fawning over a bloke just wasn't her. If this was what infatuation did to a girl she'd take herself off to a convent in the morning.

And yet, she walked into the library clinging to Griffin's hand, unwilling to let him go just yet.

"Where's Jasper?" Griffin asked, glancing about the room.

Sam turned from the large map of Britain on the wall. "That American girl showed up. The one with the fangs."

"Wildcat?" Finley couldn't believe it.

Sam turned his disinterested gaze her way. "Does she have fangs and black hair?"

"She does."

"Then that's her. I forget what she said she was in town for, but she said something about needing Jasper's help with something and him owing her. She made a pretty convincing argument for him to accompany her. Really laid on the guilt about a debt and how she wouldn't ask if it wasn't important. I told him to go ahead. I mean, it's not like he wanted to be here with us, right?"

He had a point, difficult as it was to hear. Maybe Jasper wanted time away. But he cared about Emily. He would want to help her. So, whatever Wildcat wanted, it had to be important.

"I wouldn't be surprised if Jasper accompanies her back to New York," Griffin commented. "I don't think he's happy here."

"He came back on his own," Finley reminded him. "That must mean something."

"Can we get back to trying to find Emily rather than fretting over Jasper?" Sam asked, rather bitingly.

"We can do both." Griffin tapped the map. "Stop growling and show us where Emily is."

Sam didn't have to be told twice. He pointed at St. Pancras on the smooth paper. "This is where Dandy delivered the crate." He slid his finger a little south. "And this is where the tracking device says she is."

"But we were already down there," Finley protested. "Both Emily and I thought we were being watched, but we didn't see a thing."

"That's because they were carefully concealed." Sam moved to the desk and unfurled a long tube of canvas. It was another map. "This is the late duke's cartography of London's underground, with secret passages and grottos marked. He recorded every detail."

Finley blinked. "Cartography?" She wouldn't have thought that word would be part of Sam's lexicon. It certainly wasn't a word she would have said, but then she hadn't been schooled alongside a duke.

Sam pointed at the St. Pancras location on this new map. Finley peered around Griffin so she could see. There, on the older, slightly faded map, was what looked like a labyrinth of corridors and rooms, great caverns and tiny burrows, plague pits and Roman ruins, train tunnels and sewer paths, all crisscrossing and lurking at different levels beneath London.

And in one of them, beneath the already underground rail line, Emily was being held hostage. Finley glanced at Griffin. This would be difficult for him, as he sometimes suffered great anxiety in enclosed spaces.

"If we access this sewer drain we might be able to sneak up on them," Griffin suggested, pointing out a small tunnel. "Provided this map is completely accurate, and we've no reason to doubt it, Emily should be very close."

It was at that precise moment that a metallic screech sounded not far from them. Finley actually jumped. Sam went white. He released the underground map, the ends immediately curling in on themselves like waves crashing onto shore.

"What was that?" Finley asked, dreading the answer.

The large bloke picked up what looked like nothing more incredible than a compass. "It's gone," he whispered.

"What's gone?"

There was fear in his dark eyes when he raised them to meet her gaze. "Emily's signal."

"You're not coming." Sam tugged on a pair of fingerless gloves and flexed his fingers. Finley had a similar pair. They were reinforced with an incredibly hard metal across the knuckles, just in case she or Sam ever felt the need to punch, oh, say a train.

Griffin, she discovered, did not like being bossed about. He had followed Sam into the weapons room, and Finley followed him. "The devil I'm not."

Sam scowled. "Pull rank if you want, you're still not coming with me. You're staying here."

Griffin glared. If eyebrows were weapons the two of them would be bleeding profusely. "Bugger you, Morgan. You do not give the orders in this house."

Sam ignored him and slid a wicked-looking dagger into the sheath on a leather strap around his hips. Finley silently applauded. Griffin was a good person, but he'd been born to privilege, and sometimes he needed a bit of that entitlement knocked out of him. He just assumed people would do what he told them because he was the Duke of Greythorne.

It was obvious Griffin despised being ignored. She would have to remember that. "Sam, do not piss me off."

A wall of blades began to tremble, each weapon shaking in its hold. The lights inside the room flickered.

Sam was unimpressed. Finley was…well, Griffin might be a little petulant, but his power was exciting. Her insides shivered at it, which just proved that her dark half was alive and well.

Heedless of the possible danger to his own flesh, Sam

plucked a small hatchet from the blade wall. "Griff, if the Machinist can make a mess of you from a distance, imagine what he can do when you're close. There's a very good chance he's going to be where Emily is. I'm not going to worry about you as well as her. You're going to stay at home with Finley."

At one time she would have argued, as well, but not now. As much as she loved Emily, protecting Griffin was more important to her. Sam would find Em and bring her home. She knew this because it was stupidly obvious that Sam loved Emily just as she loved him. The lucky fools.

Griffin, on the other hand, simply didn't want to admit he was vulnerable to the Machinist. And Finley didn't mind watching over him. If Garibaldi came back she'd be ready for him.

The rows of blades quieted. "I don't like you going down there by yourself. If Garibaldi is there, you'll be in danger. At least if I'm with you I can distract him."

"You don't have to be with me to distract him." Sam sighed. "This is wasting time. For years I've trusted your judgment and done whatever you asked of me. I was literally ripped apart, but I'm still here. That's because I trust you and believe in what we do. Now, you have to trust and believe in me."

Well done, Sam! It was so lovely to hear someone other than herself telling Griffin he needed to give the same amount of trust to his friends that he expected in return.

"I do trust you," he mumbled. "I just don't want you or Emily to get hurt."

One of Sam's large hands came down on his shoulder. "And I don't want you to get hurt, so please, stay here. Snog with Finley, and if I'm not back by morning, I'll expect the two of you and the cowboy to come find me."

Griffin nodded. It was obvious he didn't like the situation, but Finley suspected that had more to do with a sense of responsibility than control. Griffin was their leader, and he looked out for each of them. He hadn't said much about it, but he probably felt responsible for Emily's abduction in the first place. If he'd done a better job of protecting her she wouldn't have been taken. If he'd done things differently Mei wouldn't be dead. If he'd gotten rid of the Machinist the first time they wouldn't be doing this now. If...if...if... It was a wonder he didn't drive himself insane with all the responsibility he tried to take on.

"Be careful," Griffin advised. "And take one of these." From a drawer he withdrew a small metal sphere about twice the size of a marble and offered it to his friend.

Sam took it, rolling the ball in his palm before dropping it into his pocket.

"What is that?" Finley asked when it became apparent that neither of them was going to offer an explanation.

"An Aetheric field generator disruptor," Griffin told her.

She arched a brow. "Which does...?"

"It will interfere with the workings of anything automaton and sentient." It was Sam who explained. "It's useless against standard metal, but once the organites take hold, Aetheric energy is produced. The sphere is really only good against something caught between machine and human."

She almost asked if it would work on him, but caught herself. Of course it wouldn't. Sam was all human despite a few metal bits.

"What about machines that don't produce Aetheric energy?"

Sam hoisted a large, double-headed hammer from a rack on the floor. There wasn't a hint of fear anywhere in his expression, and part of Finley responded to that with a desire to do violence. His muscles bulged as he housed the weapon over his shoulder. He resembled the woodcutter in those fairy stories who was supposed to kill the heroine but helped her instead, or dispatched the big bad wolf.

"I can handle those on my own."

And she believed him.

Chapter 13

Emily woke up when someone crawled into the cot with her, tipping the tiny bed to the side.

"Sam?" The moment she said his name she knew it wasn't him. Sam would never do such a thing. Fear slammed hard into her chest. She was without a weapon, but she wasn't defenseless. She flipped over, fingers curving into eyeball-raking claws.

"Who's Sam?" Mila asked, catching Emily's wrist as though her strike was no more effectual than a leaf on the wind.

Relief washed over her—more potent than the pain in her arm. Mila needed to learn a better sense of her own strength, but Emily wasn't going to hold a grudge.

"A friend," she replied, gently pulling free of the girl's grip. "You shouldn't sneak up on people like that."

"Sorry, but I had to wake you."

Emily propped herself up on her elbow and peered into the darkness where she reckoned Mila's head should be. "Is something wrong, lass?"

Light flared. Mila held a small lantern that looked to have been made out of a jam jar and various other bits of refuse. She set it on the bed between them and then opened her left hand.

In her palm were the remains of Emily's spider—the very one she'd spied earlier. It was just a machine—she could build another—but she felt the loss of it keenly. Had it managed to send her location home before being destroyed?

"Why did you do that?" she asked.

"Because Her Majesty saw it and didn't recognize it. I was afraid of what she might do when she realized what it was and that it was yours."

She supposed she ought to thank Mila for her consideration, but she couldn't find it within herself. By now the machines would have gathered the items needed to start the transplant. If her friends didn't find her soon then she would have no choice but to start the process and then kill Garibaldi. The moment she did that her own life would be forfeit. She didn't mind dying to prevent the Machinist from walking free…correction, she minded it well enough, but she was willing to sacrifice herself if she could take him with her.

"Get up and grab your things," Mila instructed, climbing off the cot. "We're leaving."

This was an unexpected turn of events. "*We* are?"

In the lamplight the girl looked fierce—and a lot like Finley. "I may have been built rather than born, but I will eventually be every inch as real as you are. I have a heart that beats, lungs that breathe. I have a voice. A mind. The man in that vat is not my master and I will not be his flesh suit."

The words *flesh* and *suit* were two that never should be used together, Emily thought with a grimace. But if Mila came with her, then Garibaldi would be vulnerable, and if he didn't die on his own, he probably would once the proper authorities were called in. At the very least he'd be kept in a cell for the rest of his days.

The authorities would want to study Mila, which was another reason Emily couldn't leave her. The girl hadn't quite learned to lie, and she was too open for her own well-being. Anyone who talked to her long enough would find out exactly what she was, and then they'd find out about the organites. They might discover her connection to Griffin, as well. And that might bring people sniffing around King House, which was the last thing they needed.

But those weren't the most important reasons to take Mila with her back to King House. The simple fact was that in this brief amount of time, Emily had formed an attachment to her. She felt responsible for her, as she might a younger sibling. She had to protect her.

Emily pulled on her boots. She'd gone to sleep in her clothes—she was safer that way—and grabbed some tools she couldn't bear to leave behind. She had no problem stealing them, as they were top-notch, and more than likely had been used by Garibaldi himself.

"All right," she murmured. "Let's go. Do you know how to get us out of here?"

Mila nodded. "Follow me." She extinguished the lantern, but when the cell door opened and the dim light from the corridor filtered in, Emily detected a subtle glow in the girl's eyes. They were like a cat's. Was that left over from her construction, or something new the organites had given her? They were the beginning of all life, and responsible for the evolutionary mutations occurring in people as well as machines. With the amount of "evolved" organites that made up

Mila's genetic code it was no surprise that she might have begun to evolve in her own way.

Every mutation just made her that more dangerous, and that much more in need of protection.

Down the rough corridor they crept. There was just enough light for Emily to see one foot in front of the other. She held the leather bag with her few belongings close to her body in case a grasping hand came out of the darkness.

They had to skirt the chamber where Garibaldi slumbered. "Victoria" sat in her chair, "plugged into" the Machinist's tube. Emily could smell the rank deterioration of her flesh, see the further evidence of decay.

Soon, her metal skeletal system would begin to show through the rotting skin. She'd feel for the creature if it hadn't abducted her.

That made her think of the big spider with the awful doll head. Where was it? She raised her gaze and saw it—tucked into a corner in the ceiling. Had it seen them? No, it was sleeping; she could hear its snores— the only noise other than the instruments in the lab. The other automatons who were sentient must also be resting. The others would have been powered down.

Mila had moved ahead and Emily quickened her pace to catch up. The girl had longer legs and far more grace than she ever would. That was courtesy of Jasper, she reckoned.

A loud bubbling noise turned her head. Garibaldi moved in his tank, as though caught in the throes of a nightmare.

Mary and Joseph. Were his eyes open?

Her companion opened a door and hissed at her—a gesture for her to hurry up. Clutching the bag tight so it wouldn't rattle, Emily sprinted over the threshold, heart hammering.

They were in the catacombs where she and Finley had come. She remembered passing by this very spot. As the door closed behind them, she turned to examine it. There was barely a seam in the wall, and a small grate at eye level that a person would miss if they weren't looking for it. That explained why she'd felt as though someone was watching them—someone had been.

"Is this what the world looks like?" Disappointment practically dripped from her tongue.

Emily smiled. How could she not? "No. This would be just a wee part of it." The girl was in for a huge surprise once they made it street-side. She reached out and took Mila's hand in hers. "Come on then, the exit's this way."

Side by side they hurried down through the dark

passage. They made a turn into a tunnel that was much brighter lit than the one they were currently in. "That's our way out," Emily said, squeezing Mila's fingers.

The girl squeezed back. Emily gritted her teeth. What a bloody strong grip!

As they neared their exit, a man appeared ahead of them. Mila froze, pushing Emily behind her. "Stay back."

Emily stumbled around her. "Wait. I think I... Sam?"

"Em?"

A ragged sob caught in her throat. He had come for her, just as she knew he would. She bolted toward him. His steps quickened, closing the distance between them. She grinned like an idiot. She'd never been so happy to see him.

Sam's grin faded as he glanced past her. He reached for her. "Get down!" he yelled as he seized her by the arms and thrust her out of the way. Emily spun into the wall, the rough stone scraping her cheek. Out of the corner of her eye she saw something lunge at Sam.

The smell should have alerted her. It was "Victoria" and she wasn't alone. Several machines closed in on them. Mila was already fighting two. She might have needed to learn how to read, but she certainly didn't need to learn how to fight.

Sam pulled a large hammer from his back—the kind workmen used to knock through walls. Holding it with both hands, he swung hard and fast. It connected with the Victoria automaton's head with a sickening clanging-squish sound.

The head rolled to a spot not far from Emily's feet. There was a little blood, but it was old and the flesh was split, the head completely caved in on one side. Gray matter leaked onto the ground. Emily was not a squeamish person—she'd performed surgeries on people— but that disembodied head lying rotten and open...the smell...

She wretched. Her stomach was empty, and the bitter taste of bile gripped her tongue. She forced herself to move. The Victoria automaton's body still fought, even though the head was gone, presenting a horrific sight. Sam hammered at it until it fell, and then brought the weapon down hard for one final blow.

"Get out of here," he growled at Emily, his face splattered with gore. Hoisting the hammer, he approached the oncoming machines.

He didn't seriously expect her to leave him, did he? To leave Mila? She was made of stronger stuff than that. She had her honor, and she would not turn tail and run like a bloody coward. "I'm not leaving."

Sam struck another automaton and pulled a small sphere from his pocket. She recognized it immediately.

"Mila!" she cried, running to the girl, who had knocked one of the machines across the cavern and was taunting another. "You have to get out of here." At least out of the radius of that little metal ball, or her remaining automaton systems would shut down, and Emily didn't know if that would cause irreparable damage or not.

But it was too late. Sam had already thrown the device into the fray. It beeped three times and then *vrrrroosh!*

Three of the ten remaining machines instantly shut down, falling limp where they stood.

Mila was not one of them. Emily's heart gave a sharp thump. Mila was more human than machine now.

And so was that bloody doll-headed spider. A living creature with no conscience and terrible strength. It leaped on Sam with deadly grace. The lad snapped one of the creature's limbs like a twig. The spider screamed—a high screech that felt like spikes being driven into her ears.

The ground beneath Emily's feet began to quake. Thud. Thud. Thud. Measure. Rhythmic.

Footsteps.

Slowly, she turned her head to gaze farther down the corridor—into the dark. The footfalls became steadily louder, the ground trembling. The grinding of metal joints, beginning to rust, joined in as a shadow began to emerge from the dark.

It was huge—at least twelve feet high, the top of it just inches lower than the ceiling of the tunnel. It was solid, made of what looked to be sheets and rods of iron carefully crafted and welded together. It had been devised to build train tracks underground, and it was very much like the machine that had killed Sam.

She'd saved him once from one of these monsters; she would not lose him to one now. Emily's fists clenched as she decided to stay and fight. A flicker of movement caught her attention and she looked down.

The Victoria automaton's eyes were open. No, they were *blinking*. Blinking at exactly the same time the small light on the front of the digger flashed.

They were communicating. There were no visible connections so it had to be through the Aether. Why hadn't the decaying automaton shut down when the sphere went off? Or was it now receiving power from the behemoth? The big machine must have been out of detonation radius—that was the only explanation. Unless…unless Garibaldi had somehow found a way to control his "children" through the Aether. Was he powerful enough to withstand the sphere's power?

As the mechanical beast drew closer, she spied what looked like a large pickle jar in its torso. It was filled with a greenish goo that bubbled and churned. It looked just like the stuff Garibaldi "slept" in inside his tank. "Victoria" had plugged herself into that tank to communicate with the Machinist.

Was her wild suspicion correct? Was Garibaldi controlling these machines?

As if answering her question the thing's "hands" came up, the large, serrated shovels of each half snapping together like lobster claws. The thing was headed right for Sam, which was proof that the bloody thing was in Garibaldi's control. He knew about the attack. He knew what the sight of such a machine might do to Sam.

"Get out!" she shouted at Mila. She knew what she had to do, but this was all for nothing if the girl didn't escape.

Mila looked bewildered. "I can't leave you!"

"You have to! Go, now!" Emily picked up a large brick and tossed it to her. Mila coshed her opponent with it until the machine clattered to the floor. And then—with only a moment's hesitation—she ran toward the light, toward the exit. One of the automatons followed her, but it wouldn't get far if it went topside.

Emily turned her attention back to the digger lumbering toward Sam. Garibaldi was going to kill him; she knew this without a doubt. She didn't think, she simply acted. It was the kind of behavior she normally chastised Sam and Finley for, but now she understood it. That bone-deep reaction to someone you love being in mortal danger.

Sam turned as she ran toward the machine. The huge spider had four of its legs wrapped around him and was attacking with the others. He was bleeding but still standing. Another machine struck the back of his knees, buckling them, taking Sam to the ground. The digger moved faster, eager to stomp him with its huge feet.

She jumped.

"Emily!" Sam's cry echoed in the dank darkness. She didn't even look. She couldn't be distracted, not now. The sole of her boot came down on the digger's thigh. She used that momentum to propel herself onto its back. Great arms swung, trying to reach her, but she flattened herself against the metal, warmed by the machine's engine.

Her feet found the footholds maintenance workers would use to make repairs. She used these for balance as her fingers pried open the panel high in the center of the digger's back. It was stuck hard, and she had to pull with all her strength.

The panel flew open. Emily dug her heels in and managed to keep hold of the panel door so she didn't fall off. The digger was almost to Sam, who was trying to struggle to his feet with four automatons battering him.

The digger pivoted as Emily drove her hand into its control center. The stone wall came flying toward her as the machine sped backward. She leaped up, grabbing the digger's head and just managed to avoid being crushed to death by wrapping her legs around the monstrosity's head.

"Em!"

She peered around the digger as it jerked sideways toward Sam. He rose to his feet despite the amount of metal trying to drag him back down. "I'm fine!" she yelled. Quickly, she maneuvered her body into position so she could hang upside down, her feet locked around the machine's neck as she faced its back.

Emily drove her hands into the panel. It didn't really matter where. She could have attempted to use her abilities just by touching the external shell, but getting inside worked better, and she didn't want to take any chances with this one since she didn't even know if this would work.

It would work, or she'd die trying. Sam would not die today—and not any other day that she was alive to prevent it.

Her fingers wrapped around wires, were scraped raw and pinched by gears. The rough edge of the digger's shovels tried to grab her legs, but succeeded only in ripping her trousers. Pain radiated up her thigh as the skin there tore open.

Do you really believe you can stop me, child?

Emily froze. Garibaldi?

Who else? You could join me, Miss O'Brien. Your talents are wasted with the young duke, and not even you will be able to save him from me. You know that, don't you? I will crush him just as I'm about to crush young Samuel. I'll destroy them all, and you can't stop me. Not even you are strong enough to do that.

She clenched her jaw as she jostled on the thing's back. Garibaldi was trying to distract her. "You talk too much," she growled, then reached down inside herself and *pushed*.

The digger stumbled. She clamped her legs tighter so she didn't fall off.

What are you doing?

"I reckon I'm believin' I can stop you after all, you son of a bitch." She gripped the internal workings all the harder and released that switch deep inside herself that held her power in check. She had no idea how strong she was, or if she could even affect this monster, but it wasn't a machine on the verge of becoming sentient— it was just a machine being psychically controlled by a bloody madman.

It was like a wave of ice, or perhaps a jet of fire roaring up from her belly. It both froze and burned her chest and arms, erupting out of her hands with such force sparks of light danced before her eyes.

"Emily!" It was Sam. Gorgeous, stubborn Sam. He'd come for her. Emily smiled as darkness flooded her vision. She couldn't feel anything but the cold burn in her hands. Couldn't see. Couldn't speak.

And then she was falling and there was nothing at all.

Mila jerked to a stop at the top of the steps, her mouth dropping open. All around her people bustled about, metallic horse hooves hitting the cobblestones as wheels clattered behind. Motor carriages zipped past puffing steam and adding their own unique sound to the cacophony that was London.

She'd never seen the city before. In fact, she had no memory of anything other than her crate and the space below.

It was beautiful. It smelled of dirt and flesh and food and horse, and there was a whiff of sewer in the air, mixed with coal dust. Even as she wrinkled her nose she breathed more of it in. How had humans managed to build such an amazing place? How did they function with so much distraction around them?

A clicking on the stairs behind her caught her attention, and she turned in time to see a tall, thin automaton coming after her. It looked like a doll with no face or hair, just smooth, tarnished metal, and a ragged slash where a human mouth would be. Gears ground and clicked at her. It was trying to talk, she realized, but hadn't evolved enough to form words, poor thing. How did it even see her?

"Go back," she told it. "You don't belong up here."

It ignored her and continued its awkward ascent. What did it hope to do to her? She was stronger, surely. Sturdier.

And then she saw its hands—its curved, taloned ap-

pendages that shone in the lamplight. Those long claws
could rip her open like a fish belly. How did she know
how easy it was to slice open a fish?

It hardly mattered. She couldn't just stand there and
wait for the thing to take a swipe at her. Mila turned
and began to run. "Automaton!" she yelled, voice
rough. "There's an automaton on the loose!"

Around her people stopped and stared. Frightened,
excited voices rose up as the metal emerged from the
underground. It started down the street after her, running with an odd, hobbled gait. Women screamed.
Men swore. It didn't matter that it was late at night, a
crowd gathered regardless. A shrill whistle cut through
the night. The police, she thought. That's what that
whistle meant.

She did not want the police, she knew this. They
would want to know who she was and where she was
from, and those were questions she couldn't answer
truthfully without them either locking her up or giving her to someone for study. No, the coppers couldn't
help her, but she knew someone who could.

All the knowledge she had—even that which she
wasn't aware of having—was part of her programming,
both mechanical and organic. She'd been built to have

certain skills and abilities, but the human tissue used to construct her flesh, organs and mind—the stuff that had sparked the growth of her soul—imparted her with much of the same knowledge as those who were now a part of her. She understood all of this without any real idea of how, and her still-developing brain couldn't offer up any reason why except that it was all true.

She ran east and a bit south. Instinctively, she kept to back streets and alleys, those dark places where there were few people and even fewer who cared why a young woman would be running through the night in ill-fitting clothes and no shoes, at a speed that no normal human could ever reach.

It took her approximately ten minutes to reach her destination. The exact address had come to her like a picture in her mind—a memory that originally belonged to someone else—called up by the part of her brain that had once been a logic engine, storing all the information it had ever been given.

The person at this house was part of her. He meant something to one of her female genetic contributors, but he meant something to Mila as well, though he probably had no notion of it.

She jumped from the walk to the top of the steps

and grabbed the knocker. The bloody thing came off in her hand, splinters of wood flying. *Oops.* What was she supposed to do now? Tentatively, she raised her fist and knocked—gently—on the door. It opened a few seconds later.

He stared at her. Mila stared back. He was, quite frankly, the most beautiful thing she'd ever seen. The sight of him made the lump of meat in her chest pound with such force it hurt. Breath caught in her throat as she forgot how to breathe. A girl could be quite happy to do nothing but stare at a face like his all day.

"Do you know who I am?" she asked.

He nodded—warily. Dark eyes peered up the darkened street and then down before focusing on her once again. "I know you."

"Emily is in danger."

He frowned. "The little ginger?"

She nodded. She wasn't quite sure what ginger meant, but she knew it fit, just as she'd instinctively known that he would know exactly who Emily was. "Will you help me?"

He stood back so that she could enter the house. "I'll do what I can, Poppet. I suppose I owe you that much."

She stepped over the threshold and held out her hand. "Thank you. I'm Mila."

Warm, surprisingly strong fingers curved around hers as he pushed the door closed with his other hand. His gaze locked with hers, and she felt a jolt that shot all the way down to her toes. Was that normal? Or was she experiencing some sort of malfunction?

"Welcome to my home, Mila. You can call me Jack. Now, why don't you tell me everything that's happened since I left you underground."

Chapter 14

Finley normally counted Griffin among the smartest people she'd ever known or ever would, but at three o'clock that morning she entertained the notion that he was quite possibly the most thickheaded and dimwitted example of humanity she'd ever had the misfortune to stumble over.

"Let me get this straight," she began, wiping sleep from her eyes. "You haven't had a nightmare about Garibaldi tonight so you're afraid that means Sam and possibly Emily are dead?"

"It has to mean *something*," he insisted. "The dreams started after our return from New York and have become increasingly more frequent. Every dream for the past week has had something to do with him, and now nothing. It's not right."

She yawned. Normally she was a night person, but concern for Emily—and for Griffin—had disrupted her sleep as of late. She should be worried about Griffin right now—concerned for his sanity, but she was too tired and a little too vexed. Why did he have to come calling when she'd only been asleep—she checked the clock beside her bed—for one hour and forty-two minutes? Tomorrow night she'd lock her door, not that it would do her any good when he owned the key to it and every other room in the house.

"Why can't you just be thankful for a dreamless night?" she asked. "Or, if that's too much, then why not go back to bed and see what happens? There are still a few hours before the sun comes up."

He gave her a very annoyed glance. Oh, how she wanted to stick her tongue out at him in return!

"I'm telling you something is wrong."

"Of course something is wrong. Emily's missing, Sam has gone to find her, and Jasper is off with Wildcat. Our entire group is fractured."

"Sam should have been back by now."

"He told us to wait until morning before looking for him."

"It's morning now."

"It's still bloody dark!" She hadn't meant to speak so loudly—the servants didn't need to hear them harping on one another. She sighed, forcing herself to be calm, drawing serenity through the runes Griffin had tattooed on her skin. Whether or not they actually soothed her was still a mystery, but she liked to think they did.

Griffin turned away from her, hands on his lean hips. Finley climbed out of bed and went to him, heedless of the fact that she wore only a pair of bloomers and a camisole, while he was almost completely covered by a black dressing gown. She'd seen him naked, so she was still ahead in that respect. She wasn't cold, thanks to her natural body temperature running on the warm side. She didn't hesitate to reach out and touch his shoulder. He didn't pull away, but he didn't face her, either.

"I know you're worried," she began. Did she sound patronizing? "I'm worried, too."

"I'm bloody powerless," he replied, voice hoarse. "They're my friends, Fin. I let them down. I…"

"You have got to stop taking responsibility for everything that happens to all of us. It's not only impossible, but completely mad to even try. Not to mention how vexing it is for the rest of us. Griffin, please. I need you, and I'm scared of what might happen if you don't start worrying about yourself as much as you do everyone else."

Slowly, he turned. Her hand remained on his shoulder, and there was just enough room for her bent elbow between them. The skin under his eyes looked slightly bruised, and there was stubble on his jaw. It made him look older, and a little dangerous. Her heart rolled over when their gazes locked.

Griffin reached out and curled a lock of her hair around his fingers. She'd somehow developed two swaths of black in her hair shortly after meeting Griffin. It had bothered her at first, but now she liked it.

"You need me, eh?"

Finley nodded. His other hand splayed across her back, fingers warm through her thin linen camisole. All the moisture in her mouth disappeared, leaving her a little short of breath, her face flushed.

His chest was bare beneath the dressing gown. She could see his skin in the dim light, smell his soap and his warmth. Her hand slid down to rest just over his heart. Its rhythm was strong against her palm, the muscle there firm beneath her fingers.

It took all of her will to push him away. "I do, but

I'm not going to be a distraction for you, or allow you to be one for me."

"A distraction?" He folded his arms across his chest. "Is that what you think you are? That I am? Bloody hell, woman. I need something to distract me *from* you! Why do you think I feel so guilty about Emily and Sam? It's because I don't even think of them when I'm with you. All I can think about is how you smell and feel, that I want to kiss you and touch you and..." He looked away.

Heart in her throat, Finley took a step toward him. "And?"

Griffin's head turned just enough that he could look at her from the corner of his eye. His jaw was tight. "You know what. Two of my best friends are in trouble, and all I want right now is you. You think I'm proud of that?" He laughed humorlessly. "You're not a distraction, you're a bloody obsession."

Oh. Those words might have been said harshly, but they tied her insides up in joyful knots. What was the correct response? *Thank you* felt a bit weak. Throwing herself into his arms and kissing him until his lips were chapped seemed a bit excessive. Not to mention kisses would only be more of a distraction from the current problem.

Finley was saved having to say anything by a sound from the balcony outside her room. She and Griffin shared a surprised but suspicious look. Amorous feelings forgotten, Finley snatched up her dressing gown and slipped it on, tying the sash tight around her waist.

She moved to the French doors. She couldn't see out because the drapes were closed, so she reached out and silently—quickly—opened the door.

Jack stood before, hand raised to knock. He seemed as surprised to see her as she was to see him. He grinned. "Good ear, Treasure. I must be losin' me touch."

Did he realize how close she was to swiping that toothsome grin off his handsome face? Lord, she'd thought he was an automaton or some other sort of villain!

"What are you doing here, Jack? And why climb to my balcony when you could have used the front door?"

"I've something of a somewhat delicate nature to discuss and didn't want to wake the servants."

"It couldn't wait till morning?"

He brushed past her to enter the room. "I'm wounded. Not like I haven't opened my door to you at an ungodly— Oi, evenin', Your Grace."

Finley had been too peeved to notice that Jack hadn't

been using his usual Cockney affectation until he slipped back into it at the sight of Griffin. She turned from the door to find the two blokes facing each other like gladiators about to fight to the death.

"You make a habit of entering young ladies' rooms, Dandy?" Griffin inquired with a scowl.

"Least I'm fully clothed, Monsieur *le duc*." He fluttered his eyelashes coyly. "Don't get your unmentionables in a twist. I knows where my darlin' Treasure keeps 'er heart, and it ain't wiv me. Besides, I'm 'ere to see you as much as she."

This admission didn't surprise Finley. However, she noted that it did seem to surprise Griffin. Was it awful that she sometimes enjoyed his jealousy where Jack was concerned? It didn't hurt to have him think another fellow sought her attention.

"It's late, Jack," she reminded him, breaking up their staring contest before one of them decided to mark her as his territory. "Please, enlighten us as to what brings you calling at this hour."

"Right. First of all, my apologies for interruptin' your...whatever you were doing. I 'ad a visitor come callin' earlier, and I figured you lot would want to know of it."

"Who was it?" Griffin demanded.

Jack's eyes narrowed. "Impatient bugger, aren't you? I could tell you, but I reckon it's best that I introduce you." He raised his chin and his voice. "Oh, Poppet! Be a love and come in, will you?"

The balcony door opened. Finley whipped around to confront this new guest and found herself staring into her own eyes set in a different face. She drew back.

The girl had Emily's hair, but her complexion was a little darker. Her mouth looked like Jasper's only more feminine. Her nose—well, her nose looked like Griffin's, but smaller, and she had his foolishly long eyelashes, too. These things hit her all at the same time; they were so obvious. Though, she might not have noticed them were it not for those uncanny eyes.

Griffin came to stand beside her so they could both inspect this stranger.

"You're one of his," Griffin murmured. It didn't sound so much an accusation as a realization.

The girl nodded, eyes wide.

"Mila, make the acquaintance of Miss Finley Jayne and the Duke of Greythorne, Griffin King." Jack leaned his shoulder against one of the bedposts as he spoke. "Mila is the reason that darlin' little ginger was taken from your collective bosom and trussed up in an underground lair. 'Parently she was supposed to put some bloke's brain in Mila's noggin."

"The Master," Mila amended. "Her Majesty wanted to put his brain in my head, but Emily wasn't going to let them."

"Her Majesty?" Finley turned her attention to Griffin. "The Victoria automaton?"

Griffin shrugged. "Wouldn't surprise me. It wasn't found in the warehouse wreckage." A muscle in his jaw flexed as it always did when he blamed himself for something. He'd been doing that a lot lately.

She turned back to the girl—and there was no denying that this was indeed a living, breathing girl. She didn't remember seeing an unfinished female form at the warehouse, but that didn't mean anything. Garibaldi could have had her stashed elsewhere. Or, perhaps she was new.

"Your master used our genetic material to make your flesh, didn't he?"

"Not him specifically—he's in a revitalizing chamber—but Her Majesty and the others did as he instructed."

Jack finally stepped up to join them. "A revitalizin' chamber, for those of you who may not be familiar with such a rig, is a big-arse tank filled with human gooey bits and other delicious substances to 'eal injuries and sustain life."

Griffin shot him a wry glance. "I know."

Jack made a face. "I suppose you 'as one in your loo, 'aven't you, dukey? Keeps you lookin' all youthful and fresh for the ladies."

Dandy was in fine form tonight, Finley thought. Was it because he assumed she and Griffin had been… intimate? Or was it because he'd been drawn into this mess? Maybe he felt a little guilty for being the one to deliver Mila to those who kidnapped Emily. Regardless, it was annoying.

"Play nice, boys," she warned. "You want to butt heads, take it outside. Are you hungry?" she asked Mila.

The girl nodded. "I am."

"Let's get you fed then. You can tell us everything while you eat."

"And you'll save Emily and Sam?"

Finley paused, resisting the urge to look to Griffin. "Yes. We will save them."

She smiled, an expression that was entirely her own. Finley took her by the hand. "Come with me."

They'd only made it two steps when Mila dug in her heels. It was like trying to haul a steam carriage out of a bog. Finley succeeded in pulling her an en-

tire foot farther and earned a surprised look in return.
What had she said about butting heads? Griffin and Jack
were each a bad influence on her. Here she was trying
to dominate this poor, frightened thing who was still
a child in many ways.

Mila turned her torso, arching slightly as she looked
back over her shoulder at Jack. She held out her hand.
"You're coming, too, aren't you?"

A flicker of refusal glinted in Jack's dark eyes, but it
was soon replaced by a gentle expression that ignited
a tiny bit of jealousy in Finley's own heart. She didn't
have romantic feelings for Jack, but he was *hers*. He
knew her better than anyone, and she was supposed to
be the only one who saw this side of him.

"Course, Poppet. You'll not get rid of me that easily."

Griffin didn't protest—so that was as good as permis-
sion. The four of them made their way quietly downstairs, and then down another set to the kitchen where
Finley played hostess and put together a platter of cold
meats, cheese and bread for them to share. Mila dug in
like a ravenous dog. Jack stopped her with a hand on
her arm. "You're going to do yourself a harm, pet. Eat
slowly. There's plenty more where that come from."

Mila nodded and smiled at him. Poor thing looked
at him like her savior. Then again, he was probably the

first human she'd ever had contact with. If he hadn't opened that crate who knows what sort of mess they'd be in right now. They'd have no idea where Emily was, and Sam would have torn apart most of London looking for her.

As she ate, Mila told them about "waking up" in the catacombs, and how she remembered Jack. She related how Emily arrived and that she'd helped her learn to read. She talked about the Machinist and his plans, and she told how she and Emily had escaped, only to be set upon when Sam arrived. She was very impressed with Sam's destruction of Her Majesty. Finley wished she'd been there to see it. She should have crushed that thing's head when she had the chance.

Mila also told them about the digger and that Emily had told her to run, so she had. Finley's chest tightened as she turned her gaze to Griffin's. He'd gone pale, and while his expression was bleak, his eyes burned with anger.

The pots on the wall shook. The stove rattled. Even the floor beneath their chairs trembled.

"Do you mind, mate?" Jack asked. "This sort of thing wreaks havoc on me digestion."

For a second Finley feared that Griffin might tear

Jack apart from the inside out. Instead, everything went still and Griffin actually looked relieved. "Thanks."

Jack smiled slightly. "No worries. Now, what do we do from here?"

"We?" Griffin echoed.

"I feel partially responsible for this muck up. 'Twould be ungentlemanly of you not to allow me to help set it to rights."

"Right," Griffin agreed, obviously amused. Then, he said seriously to Mila, "I suppose they'll come looking for you."

Finley watched the girl's eyes widen. It was so disconcerting seeing her own eyes in another face. "But they won't. The Master didn't want a female body, and now that they have a human male, that's the one he'll choose."

Horror clutched at Finley's heart. The Machinist wouldn't. Yes, the bastard would. It would be not only revenge on all of them, but it would be the greatest injury to Griffin. One glance at him and she knew he thought the same thing.

"Sam."

Mila and Jack waited downstairs while Finley and Griffin dressed. Jack reclined on the sofa like a lazy cat, one leg on the cushions, the other over the side. Mila walked around the perimeter of the room, mouth suspended in an O of awe. Every wall, right up to the ceiling, was lined with shelf after shelf of books. She couldn't imagine reading all of them, and yet she would love to try.

"You could sit down, Poppet."

"I don't feel like being still." She turned her head toward him. "Have you ever seen so many books in one place?"

Jack nodded. "It's common for rich nobs to have extensive libraries. Thinks it makes them look learned. I doubt His Grace has read even half of these."

She stopped looking at the leather-bound books to face him. "You talk differently with me. Why?"

He slipped his arm beneath his head and closed his eyes. He looked like the very definition of languid. "Can you keep a secret, Poppet?"

"I don't know. I've never had to keep one before." And then, "What's a poppet?"

Jack didn't open his eyes, but he smiled. "It's an endearment. A nickname."

Endearment. That meant it was said with affection. "Are you going to tell me your secret? I promise to do my best to keep it."

He chuckled. He had a nice laugh. "Sometimes it suits me to sound posh and other times I need to sound not so posh."

"Isn't that lying?"

"Not if what I say is the truth."

That really wasn't much of an answer. Even though she was almost completely human now, she still had much to learn about what it was to *be* human. She had a sinking feeling learning that was going to be more difficult than learning to recognize words and their meanings.

"That girl—Finley—has the same eyes as me."

"Yes. You remind me a little of her."

"You care for her very much." Griffin obviously felt the same. And then there was Sam, who came to rescue Emily. How did it feel to matter that much to someone? The only person she meant anything to just wanted her to be his vessel, and even then he'd replaced her easily enough.

"She's my friend." His eyes opened. "Do you understand friendship?"

"I think so. I feel fondness for Emily. I'm concerned for her safety."

"That sounds like friendship to me."

"Do you think we'll save them?"

"If anyone can it's this lot. His Grace is a bit of a git, but he'll do whatever's necessary to bring them home."

"Home." Mila ran her hand down a line of books. "It must be nice to have a place where you belong."

Jack's eyes opened, and he turned his dark gaze on her. "Sometimes you have to make that place for yourself."

"Oh, he has *Pinocchio!*" She took the book from the shelf and opened it. The words were gibberish to her. Panic welled up in her chest. "I can't read it! I don't understand."

Jack gracefully sat up, swinging his leg off the sofa to rise in one fluid movement. He walked over to her and took the book from her hands. "It's written in Italian," he told her.

Italian. That was another language. Mila paused a moment to search her brain before reclaiming the book back from Jack. When she looked at it now the words made sense. Grinning, she read a passage of it aloud, and looked up to find Jack watching her with an odd expression on his face. She wasn't very good with expressions yet. Smiles and frowns were easy, but reading a face like his would require more skill and practice. He looked as though he could be somewhat disgusted, amazed or, perhaps, constipated.

She opened her mouth to ask which but was stopped by Griffin and Finley's arrival.

"Your Italian is very good," Griffin praised. Mila knew she should think of him as "His Grace" but she couldn't do that. She could call him by the title, but it just seemed…foolish. Really, what was a title but a fancy nickname? Being called "Her Majesty" hadn't kept that old woman automaton from getting her head knocked off.

"Thank you. I just realized I know it."

Finley arched a brow. "I wish I had such a talent."

Did she find it as odd looking at Mila as Mila found it looking at her? Their eyes were exactly the same.

Griffin approached Mila with a gentle smile. "I assume you'll discover many new things over the next few months. I suspect your logic engine had a capacity for learning, and that the organites caused it to not only copy bits of the genetic material introduced to your construct, but to learn from them, as well."

Mila stared at him. What were organites? As soon as she thought the question, the answer came to her. She frowned. "This is very…confusing."

"I imagine it is," Griffin sympathized. "Once we've dealt with Garibaldi, we'll turn all our attention to finding out what you're capable of, and how you can access that knowledge."

"She's not a specimen for you to poke at," Jack informed him, putting himself between the duke and Mila.

She put her hand on his shoulder. "That's not what he meant, Jack. He wants to help me."

High black brows pulled tight and low over fathomless eyes. "You're too trusting."

Was he angry with her or defending her? She was going to assume the latter given how he used his lean body to shield her. "No, I'm not. I know them. I can't explain it, but I know he's not lying to me."

Griffin directed his attention to Jack. "It could be a side effect of the genetic bonding."

Jack snorted. "Or it could be a powerful peer of the realm taking advantage of an innocent girl."

The two stared at each other—two alphas vying for dominance.

"You went to Eton, didn't you?" Griffin asked. "Who are you really, Jack Dandy?"

Mila noted that Finley seemed as eager to hear the answer to that as Griffin. She wanted to know, too. There was no hint of Jack in her head, or soul. He was not part of the genetic stew that made her who she was. Perhaps that was what made him so very interesting.

"The son of an innocent girl taken advantage of by a powerful peer," Jack replied tightly, lifting his chin. She didn't have to be connected to him to realize this was something he expected to be judged by. She wasn't certain of the full implication of his words because the context didn't quite make sense to her, but she did notice the caring and sympathetic expression Finley wore as she looked at Jack. Mila—for reasons she could not deduce—wanted to march over and pinch her as hard as she could.

Griffin extended his arm and offered his hand to Jack. "I give you my word that I will not allow Mila to come to harm."

Jack accepted the handshake. "Thanks, but 'tisn't me who needs to hear that promise."

Finley sighed—loudly. "If you two are finished posturing, I'd like to go rescue my friends."

Cheeks flushing, Griffin nodded. "Finley's right. Emily and Sam are what matters now. Mila, do you think you can lead us back to the Machinist's lair?"

"When you say 'Machinist' you mean the man I was told was my master, don't you?" At his nod, she added, "Yes. I know exactly where it is."

"Excellent." Griffin walked over to the wall and pulled one of the books off the shelf, turned it around and put it back into place.

The wall of books split down the middle and pulled apart to reveal a most impressive collection of devices humans used to kill one another.

Mila watched as Jack approached. "My opinion of you just improved, Your Grace."

"My name is Griffin. If we have to trust one another not to let the other die, I prefer to have a degree of familiarity."

Mila didn't know what all of this nonsense was about. She only had one name—well, other than Endeavor 312. However, she sensed that this was a very important moment between Griffin and Jack.

Jack took what looked like a stick...what was the word? *Cane.* He took what looked like a gentleman's cane from the wall. Holding the silver topper with one hand, he gave it a twist and pulled. A thin, glimmering sword came free with a *whisssk.*

He made a sound of approval. "May I?" he asked Griffin.

The young man nodded. "Of course."

"Oh, for heaven's sake!" Finley sighed and went to

the wall where she grabbed a few small items. Then, she went to Mila.

"Here," she said, offering some of the items. "These will protect the skin over your knuckles."

Mila took them. There was a space to put her fingers through. "Thank you. Is your corset metal?"

"Yes. It's like armor."

"Do I get one?"

Identical gazes met. "Your armor is inside." The girl put her hand over Mila's torso. "Feel that hardness beneath your skin and muscle? That's metal, and it will protect your insides from injury."

Mila put her own hand on the other side. She could feel the hardness. "Real people don't have this, do they?"

"Not as a rule, no. That just makes you different. Griffin and I are different from most people, as well."

"Sam and Emily are, too, aren't they?"

"Yes."

She looked at Jack. "Are you different?"

"You don't know the 'alf of it, Poppet," he replied, phony accent back in place. Then to Griffin, "I thought we were going to rescue some people rather than stand around jabberin'?"

Mila frowned. He hadn't answered her question—
not properly.

Once they had taken up their weapons, Griffin sent
a message to someone named Jasper via a small, strange
apparatus he kept in his coat pocket. Finley gave Mila
a pair of "boots"—lovely things that covered her feet
and protected them. No more running about in bare
feet for her!

They left the house and entered a large building
where there were horses in the back and strange machines toward the front. Griffin swung his leg over one,
and Finley took another. Jack chose one that was mostly
black with bits of shiny metal. The vehicles each had
two heavy wheels and bars for steering.

"It's called a velocycle," Jack told her. He waited a
moment. "Do you know what that is?"

She did. Once he'd told her the name, she'd discovered the knowledge inside her memory. This was wonderfully convenient as well as maddening.

"Get on," he said, saving her from having to find out
if she could drive one or not.

Mila paused. "I'm too heavy for it."

Finley grinned at her. "No, you're not. That one be-
longs to Sam."

Not exactly sure what that meant, because Sam

hadn't appeared to be incredibly heavy, Mila climbed onto the velocycle behind Jack. The large frame dipped a little, but not much. Three engines roared to life at the same time. A couple of the horses whinnied.

"Hold on," Jack instructed as they took off.

The sudden burst of movement jerked her backward. Mila wrapped her arms around Jack and pressed her cheek against his back. This was not fun!

She could feel him laughing against her face and beneath her hands. Lifting her head, she dared open her eyes. The world whipped past as they sped down the darkened streets. Wind tugged at her hair and stung her eyes. She felt free.

Alive.

Perhaps this velocycle business was fun, after all.

She directed Jack to the spot where she'd come aboveground, and the others followed. Finley took the lead as they descended into the underground, Mila just behind her. Finley was very strong—she knew this because she'd actually pulled Mila when Mila hadn't wanted to move—but she had to possess more than just strength if she was the one chosen to put herself first in the path of any danger.

"What is that smell?" Finley asked, wrinkling her nose.

"That's death," Jack replied, glancing at Griffin, who nodded grimly.

"It's Her Majesty," Mila told them, her eyes adjusting to the dark so that she could see the head and mangled body lying in the shadows. "Before I ran out I remember him hitting her with something."

"A hammer," Finley supplied. She stood over what was left of Her Majesty, shining a light on the ruined mass of metal and putrid flesh.

"There's a digger." Griffin moved quickly to where the hulking machine lay. He nudged with his boot and sniffed. "Smells as though it overheated."

"You reckon it was Em?" Finley asked, glancing at him.

"Judging from the way it fell I'd say so. It was system failure not violence that took it down." He squatted beside the machine and touched its front. His fingers came away glistening with bluish-green. "This fluid has organites in it."

"It's what is in the Master's tank," Mila added.

Griffin pulled a vial from his pocket and scooped up some of the substance. "Lead on, Mila."

She led them through the dank, winding darkness. Their torches cut swaths of light through the dirt and dust. It didn't take very long to find the door to the hidden rooms. She pulled it open and stepped over the threshold. The others followed.

"What the hell…" Griffin swung the beam of his torch over the refuse and mess.

Mila couldn't believe her eyes. "They're gone."

Chapter 15

Emily's head hurt. Again. Her whole body hurt. Was she dead?

A loud clacking noise made her open her eyes a fraction. As her vision cleared she saw the doll-headed spider creature standing above her. If she was dead, she was in hell.

"She says for you to get up, you traitorous dog." The voice that spoke had a tinny sound to it. She knew without looking that it was another automaton.

"And if I don't?" she challenged, not that lying on the dirt was the least bit comfortable.

She was seized by the hair and the trousers by metal clamps and jerked to her feet. Her knees bent but held as her weight settled upon them. Her head pounded, and she pressed her hand to it. At least the machine that lifted her had released her hair.

The spider approached. It reared back on its hind legs, extending three—one was hanging bent and broken near the back four—to Emily's head and shoulders. She went rigid but didn't move as it pressed the tip of each leg to her flesh, each in a spot that ached.

Pain lanced through her and then disappeared, leaving her with a dull ache in her head rather than a raging migraine. Emily regarded the creature warily. She'd heard of this sort of treatment before but never experienced it. Supposedly the idea was to increase blood flow to and ease tension in the affected muscles. "Thank you."

It clacked at her, waving its delicate but strong limbs.

"She did not do it to be nice. She did it because we need you to be at your best."

"I don't need an interpreter," she shot back at the annoying smooth-faced automaton. "And I don't give a bloody hell how you need me."

Had they caught Mila? What happened after she took down the digger? And where was Sam? He wasn't in the room with her. What had they done with him? Panic clawed at her throat.

"For the procedure," the automaton replied as though her burst of temper hadn't mattered. It was like the one with the smooth face, only this one had a spot for eyes and a mouth built into it. "You will transfer the Master's brain into its host."

So Mila hadn't escaped. Damnation. So she would be a murderess then. No matter how this played out she was going to take a life.

She knew it might come to this. She'd already made up her mind to kill Garibaldi if the opportunity arose. No time for second thoughts now.

"Come," the metal instructed, and pushed her toward a door. It was then that she realized they were on board a train. When she crossed the narrow threshold she stepped out into a platform before entering yet another car. They weren't moving, but they were definitely on a track underground. What happened if another train came along?

Then she looked at the scene before her and she didn't care if another train crashed into them or not.

Garibaldi was still in his tank. Next to it was a sturdy cot—a surgical bed. And strapped to it with bands of steel was Sam. How much laudanum had they given him to keep him so placid?

Mila was nowhere to be seen, which meant they were keeping her elsewhere or...

Clacking. "You will put the Master's mind into this body," Metal Face told her. More clacking. "You will do this or die."

She wanted to scream at him that she understood what the damned spider said, but her throat was too tight.

On the cot Sam moved. The metal holding him groaned. A small, onion-shaped automaton depressed a syringe into Sam's neck. Within seconds he fell silent and still.

"Then I'll die," Emily said. There really wasn't any choice involved at all.

Clearly this was not what the machines expected. The spider moved around to face her, clacking so fast and sharp that it reminded Emily of her mother when she was in a fine and fierce temper.

"You will do it or *he* will die."

Emily's heart clenched. This was proof that the machines might be able to think but they couldn't feel. They didn't understand that this was even less of a threat than the one against her own life. She'd saved Sam before and made him something he didn't want to be. If she did this, his body would live but there wouldn't even be a trace of *her* Sam left in him. He would rather die than become a vessel for a man he despised—a man they all despised.

"So kill him." She looked at the spider. "I'll kill him myself if it means Garibaldi loses."

The doll head—grimy and smeared with its matted hair—turned to Metal Face. This time it chittered rather than clacked. It said something about being confused and the master. The other automaton moved gracefully across the floor. It must have been used as a server in a wealthy home or a club. It stopped at the tank and lifted a length of insulated wires, which it then plugged into the socket on the back of its skull. The metal shuddered and shook for a second and then went rigid.

A few seconds later, it spoke, "I have to say, Miss O'Brien, that you have much more of a backbone than I would have thought."

Emily's eyes narrowed. "Garibaldi." He was speaking through the automaton. "I'm never going to do what you want, so you may as well do your worst."

"You do not want me to do my worst, little girl. My worst will be crueler than you can imagine."

Really? She could imagine great cruelty. She'd already suffered more cruelty than most people in her short life.

"It must be maddening," she remarked, "having your mind so sharp and your body so utterly useless. Having to depend on your disciples to keep you alive while your agile mind plots and schemes."

"There have been some benefits. Miss Xing was quite easy to manipulate into haunting our friend the young duke, and I find the Aether most accommodating to my needs. How was Griffin last time you saw him? I imagine he's fairly exhausted by now. That makes him all the more susceptible to me, you know."

"Giving away your secrets? You must not have any intention of allowing me to survive this. That doesn't exactly motivate me, boyo." She was baiting him, but how else could she get him to admit all that he had planned? Standing around listening to his pompous ranting kept Sam alive and gave Griffin, Finley and Jasper more time to find them. And her friends would come.

"Oh, do not fret, child. I know exactly how to motivate you. You will do exactly as I command."

"Enlighten me."

Like most prideful and overly confident people he didn't need much provocation to brag about his intelligence. "You will go forward with the procedure. You will be tethered to my spider, which will be connected with my mind until the last possible moment. It will relate your progress to me. If I think for one tiny moment that you play to betray me I will make certain Griffin, Finley, that American, your brothers—everyone you care about will have a visit from my children, and they won't stop until every last one of your loved ones is dead. And you will be made to look at each and every body until you beg to be ended, as well."

Emily's mouth went dry. So much for her own arrogance. It was one thing to wager with her own life—even Sam's and the others', but to put her family at risk... Garibaldi was a top-notch villain to threaten them, and she knew he'd make good on the threat.

She needed to have a plan in place to eliminate him before the procedure began, and she wouldn't be able to think of it at all while tethered to the spider. It would pick up on any changes to her thought patterns, heart rate, et cetera.

"You will kill that many innocent people just so you can have a body?"

"Come now, you and I both know they're not that innocent. It's your fault I'm trapped like this. You played a part in my downfall. It's only fitting that you orchestrate my triumphant return."

She'd pretend to retch if Sam wouldn't suffer for it. Baiting Garibaldi was one thing, but mocking him would put him into a temper and if he was responsible for Griffin's exhaustion and lack of concentration then he might retaliate by hurting her friend all the more.

"If I do this, you will leave my family alone?"

"You have my word."

"You won't harm Griffin, Finley or Jasper, either."

He hesitated.

"Swear it, Garibaldi. I'll have your word or you can find someone else to do your bidding, and we both know you're running short on time."

"You're not in a position to provoke me, Miss O'Brien."

"You can make good on all your threats, Garibaldi, but I'm your only hope for a successful transplant. We both know that, otherwise you would have found someone else. I reckon you hadn't originally planned to let Griffin know you were still around this soon."

Silence. Yes, she had him there. He had to know that Griffin was onto him. If they hadn't realized it before Sam went missing, they would know it as soon as Mila found them, which had hopefully already happened.

The clock was ticking, which was no doubt why they were on a train rather than in the catacombs.

"Fine. I give you my word that your friends and family will not be harmed."

It didn't matter, but she breathed a sigh of relief. "Thank you. As soon as I do an inventory of surgical instruments and make certain Sam is a viable host for your mind we'll get started."

"You will start immediately. You have everything you need and Samuel has already been tested."

She must have been unconscious longer than she thought.

The spider set a pair of hair clippers on the tray next to Sam's cot. "I don't need to shave his head," she told the creature. "I can peel back his scalp to expose his skull." It was a good thing she didn't suffer from an abundance of spleen, else she'd be nauseous.

"They're for you," Garibaldi informed her through his metallic translator. "My freakish pet needs to plug into your brain."

"No, it doesn't." And did the spider mind being called a "freakish pet"? Did he not realize that his metal children could turn on him at any moment? Or was he like her and could exert his will over them? Could he do it without touching them?

"Ah, you are a Technomancer."

That was one way to describe it. A poncey way. "Yes." She didn't mind admitting it if it kept hair on her head. It was girly of her. Vain, too, but while she'd die for Sam, she would not go bald for him unless she absolutely had to.

This was not one of those times. She intended to destroy Garibaldi, and if she kept her wits about her, both she and Sam would walk out of here alive, hair and brains intact.

"Then there is no need to create a port into your mind. Lovely. That saves us so much time. Wash your hands, Miss O'Brien. You've surgery to perform."

The spider gestured to a nearby sink as the small, onion-shaped automaton wheeled over a spindly stand. They were going to have to feed Sam a steady supply of laudanum to keep him asleep throughout the entire process.

As Emily washed her hands with tepid water, she took a short moment to pray. There were times in her life when she wasn't certain God even existed. In fact, she still didn't know, but she threw her pleas for help out into the Aether and hoped that, somehow, they fell upon the right ears.

★ ★ ★

"You're mad. You know that, don't you?" Finley folded her arms over her chest. They were still underground. "Mad as a bleeding hatter."

It was obvious from the way Griffin looked at her that he didn't believe she meant it, that he was amused by it. "It's the fastest way to find Garibaldi and bring Sam and Em home."

She hated that he was right. Hated that putting himself in danger was the only plan they had. Mei was connected with Garibaldi, and Griffin figured that she would be able to locate the villain. "I'm coming in with you."

He arched a brow. "I beg your pardon?"

Finley lifted her chin. "Don't you get all haughty with me, Griffin King. If you need to be the hero, fine, but I'm not letting you do it alone."

She expected him to fight her on this. "Fine."

Now she was the one whose brow rose. "Honestly?"

"We don't have time to waste arguing, and having you with me is a sound suggestion." He held out his hand. "Come on."

"Oi, mind fillin' the rest of us in on the plan then?"

Jack leaned against the rough wall. In his head-to-toe black, he was like a shadow coming to life.

"He's going to go into the Aether," Jasper explained. He and Wildcat had arrived a quarter of an hour ago after Finley sent him a telegraph asking him to return, and for him to bring the American girl—they needed all the help they could get.

But if Wildcat thought *Finley* was going to owe her a favor for this, she was mistaken. "And then he's going to get Mei to lead him to the Machinist. Am I right?"

Griffin nodded. He held out his hand, and Jasper took it. "Thanks for joining us. I know the two of you had your own intrigue."

The American shrugged. "Emily and Sam went to another country to help me. The least I can do is show up when they're in trouble."

Finley smiled. He sounded more like the Jasper she'd come to think of as a friend. How much of the credit for that needed to be laid at Wildcat's feet?

Watching as Cat and Jack were introduced earlier had been extremely interesting. Cat was as dusky-skinned as Jack was fair. She had incredible curly dark hair and bright jade-colored eyes. She also had retractable claws and little fangs that she managed to hide. She was something of an underworld lord herself back in New York.

She and Jack seemed to understand each other in one glance. That was obvious from the way they greeted one another—with curiosity, respect and a good dose of wariness.

"Jas, do you want to go into the Aether with us?" Finley asked. He had history with Mei. He'd loved her once. Just maybe there might be some unfinished business there.

"No," the cowboy replied, casting a glance at Cat. "I said goodbye to her a while ago. No point in doin' it again."

Finley's nosy side wondered if Jasper and Cat had rekindled their romance while off on their own adventure, but that didn't matter at the moment. She needed to prepare herself for entering the Aether again. At least she knew that if something came at them she could fight it.

"You be needin' anyfing special, dukey?" Jack inquired with patently false sweetness. "Mood lightin' or the like?"

Griffin shot him a dry glance, but one corner of his mouth twitched. "Have some candles on you, Dandy? Maybe some incense?"

Finley rolled her eyes. "I swear when this is over,

I'm going to lock the two of you in a room together for a week."

"Don't make promises you don't intend to keep, Treasure. Now, be a good girl and do whatever needs to be done so we can return to civilization, will you?"

Perhaps she wouldn't lock him and Griffin in a room together. That would be too cruel to Griffin, who had just reached out and entwined his fingers with hers. "Come on, Fin. Let's get this done."

She nodded, took a deep breath and closed her eyes—it made her a little dizzy if she watched the veil separate and the two worlds merge. It was unsettling enough that the rune tattoos he'd given her tingled at the shift between dimensions. Griffin had taken her into the Aether a few times to help with the mashing together of her two personalities, and she'd been around his power enough times—gotten right in the thick of it with him—that it was easier for her to cross over. Still, it would be impossible for her to do it on her own. Like most people, she simply hadn't the talent for it.

And, honestly, it wasn't as though hanging about with dead folk was her idea of a good time. Though, someday she would like to ask Griffin about her father. He had died before she'd been born. It might be nice to meet him, if it were at all possible.

Griffin squeezed her fingers and she opened her eyes. They were in the Aether. She could see everyone watching them. To their eyes she and Griffin would be interacting with things they couldn't see, as though they acted out charades for the others to guess at. For her, it was like looking into an old, warped mirror.

"Mei?" Griffin's voice was strong in here. He sounded louder, older. How much of his soul belonged to this place already? Would she wake up one day to find that it had taken him? Or worse, that he'd given himself over to it voluntarily? How long could a human traffic in the world of the dead before it became home?

"Mei, if you can hear me I need your help."

Finley glanced around. At first she saw nothing, but then a small ripple appeared before them. The ripple grew, elongated and widened until Mei walked through it, a gray shadow of her former self.

She looked tired, battered and lost. Wasn't death supposed to be a peaceful thing? Or maybe that's what hell did to a person.

"What do you want?" she demanded.

Griffin frowned. "What happened to you?"

"Your friend decided his demons needed a new toy. He gave them me." She looked as though she blamed Griffin for her current situation.

"Look, that rots," Finley began, "but he has Sam and Emily. We need to find him."

The ghost looked as though she might start laughing. "You want me to find him for you? No. I won't. What he will do to me is worse than being trapped in a wall still alive."

Griffin didn't even wince. In fact, he didn't look the least bit sorry. "I'm not keen on going after him myself, but I have to. You will help us."

"Or what?" Mei gestured around them. "What can you do to me that's worse than this?"

"Nothing," he replied. "But if you do help us I'll personally free you from Garibaldi's control."

The girl looked dubious. Her large, dark eyes narrowed. "You can do that?"

"I can, and I will. You have my word. Will you help us?"

Mei looked around, then closed her eyes. She began to flicker in and out, like the "moving" photographs Emily liked so much. Finally, she stuttered to a stop, coming fully back to where Finley and Griffin stood.

"He is on a train beneath the city."

Griffin swore—the kind of language that made Finley arch a brow. She wasn't certain if she was alarmed or impressed. "Is it moving?"

"No. It's stopped."

He ran a hand through his hair. "At least we have that in our favor."

Mei looked back and forth between them. "He's beneath a place called Russell Square—I checked the street signs. You need to hurry. It looks like your friends are in trouble."

"What sort of trouble?" Finley asked.

"The sort that may put them here," came the flat reply. "Now shouldn't you be going? I helped you, so go help them so I can be free."

"Nice to see you've become a less selfish person," Finley commented with a sardonic smile.

Mei's eyes went totally black—no white anywhere to be seen. "He's looking for me. Go now."

They didn't need to be told twice. Finley pulled hard on Griffin's hand. "Get us out of here."

He did. Just as Mei flickered and disappeared, a black wisp no bigger than a silver dollar appeared near the spot where she'd been. It swirled like water down a drain, growing a little larger with every turn. They popped back to their proper side of the veil before it came for them.

"Do you think it saw us?" Finley asked. More importantly, had it seen Griffin? Those things had been able to attack him outside the Aether.

"I don't know. It's not in this dimension, regardless." He turned to the others. "Russell Square. Let's go."

As they left the tunnel, Griffin faced Mila. "You don't have to come with us. We'll be fighting your friends, your creator."

She met his gaze. Finley wondered if he found it odd to peer into eyes that looked like hers but weren't. Also, she wondered if her own stare ever looked quite so determined and fierce. If so, she could be deadly intimidating.

"Emily is my friend," Mila replied. "She stayed behind so I could escape. I'm going back for her."

Griffin nodded. "Fair enough." He stopped two stairs up, and pivoted to look at his followers. "Getting Emily and Sam out is our top priority. Take out any automatons that get in your way."

"What about Garibaldi?" Finley asked.

His jaw tightened, but there was an odd light in his eyes when his gaze locked with hers. "Garibaldi is mine."

Chapter 16

Sam's eyelashes fluttered. For such a rugged lad he had the girliest eyelashes—long, dark and thick. Emily's weren't nearly so long or lush, and were the color of rust beneath a layer of mud.

She knew the exact moment he regained consciousness, because his entire body tensed—so much so that the cot beneath him groaned under the stress.

"You've got to rest easy, lad," she murmured. "Don't let them know you're awake." Her entire plan rested on him being alert and able to fight as soon as she killed Garibaldi. Maybe they'd both make it out alive.

"Em?" At least he had the good sense to whisper—and he kept his eyes closed.

"Aye, it's me. I don't have much time—they'll not leave me alone with you for long. I have a plan. I may have to cut you, all right? Garibaldi has to believe I'm going to do what he wants."

"I trust you."

Her throat tightened. Did he know how much those words meant to her? Ever since he realized what she'd done to save his life they'd been at odds with each other. Oh, they still had moments of closeness, but not like before. Everything changed that night he died and she brought him back; she thought she'd lost his trust forever.

A laborer automaton—a digger—had malfunctioned. They had gone to fight it and Sam was badly hurt. Mortally so. This was before Finley joined them. Things might have been different if they'd had her on their side.

Emily blamed Garibaldi just as Sam had blamed her. He was responsible for that digger's malfunction because he'd been mucking about with organite energy cells and causing mayhem around the city.

And then he'd had the stones to try to manipulate Sam and use him against Sam's friends.

Emily cast a glance at the Machinist in his tank. He floated like a lazy swimmer in his vat of goo. Most of his face was obscured by the breathing mask he wore. It

looked as though his hair had fallen out on one side—
or that might be scar tissue.

Was it evil of her to hope that he had suffered and
suffered greatly?

Cuts and abrasions on his skin healed only to reap-
pear a little while later—she'd noticed this while studying him. The organites struggled to heal a body past
the point of repair, but they couldn't keep up with the
damage and keep vital organs functioning.

He said he'd go after the people she loved via the
Aether. Was he responsible for the attacks against Griffin in New York? With no evidence it seemed too far-
fetched to believe, but she couldn't shake the suspicion.

Threats against her life was how he managed to take
both her and Sam earlier out in the tunnels. She'd taken
down the digger, but other machines came out to play.
Emily had dropped in and out of consciousness after her
own encounter with Garibaldi's monstrous machine,
but she'd remembered hearing someone tell Sam that
if he came with them she wouldn't be hurt. When she
took the digger down she must have been immediately
set upon by more metal.

They'd been so close to escape.

How did such evil as Garibaldi even come into
being? He'd been a child once, had a mother and a

father. If she could suffer all she'd been through and still come out believing in love and the inherent goodness of man, what had happened to Garibaldi to make him so very twisted?

Her mother used to say that some people were just born bad. Perhaps that was true. The boy who had violated her came from a good family. He had friends and people who loved him. There was nothing about him that identified him as a monster.

"Em?"

She shook her head and looked down. Sam's eyes were open the tiniest fraction. "What?"

"Are you all right?"

"I will be." She gave his hand a squeeze as she heard a door open from the other car. "Back to pretending now. They're coming." Frankly, she was surprised they'd left her alone with Sam and their precious Master for this long. The machines might be sentient, but they hadn't quite figured out the art of lying. And Garibaldi was still so full of his own importance that he didn't realize that she'd kill him to protect the people she loved.

The door behind her opened, allowing a rush of damp underground in, followed by the smell of metal and machine oil.

Automatons loaded a tray beside Sam's cot with surgical instruments. Another set up lamps suspended from bent poles for better light. And the spider—the thing she'd taken to thinking of as "matron" because it seemed to boss all the others around—began fiddling with the various valves and levers on the outer panel of Garibaldi's tank. It clacked at her.

Right on cue, the faceless automaton translated, "You will begin now."

Emily nodded. Covertly, she gave Sam's arm a squeeze before moving away. "Did you get the Listerine?"

"Yes, although we do not understand the purpose of it. It is not oil. It is not used as fuel."

"It's going to keep everything clean. You wouldn't want me to put the Master's brain in this body only to have it die from infection?"

She thought she saw Sam twitch out of the corner of her eye. She would have done more than twitch if she heard someone talk about putting a new brain in her skull.

"If the Master dies, you will die, too."

"Well, then I reckon it's a fine thing that you got the Listerine." The machines might not understand lying, but they understood threats. They understood actions.

In fact, it was tempting to pick up a curved blade

from the tray and shove it underneath the thing's chin, sever its vocal cords and cut its head right off.

She was becoming as bloodthirsty as Finley. Violence was not her area of expertise.

But machines were. That was why Sam wasn't getting enough laudanum to keep him knocked out even though it looked as though he was; she'd had a little "chat" with the pump. It, thankfully, had yet to develop a mind of its own.

"You know what I don't understand about all this?" she said innocently as she began to prep and clean instruments. "Is why a bunch of intelligent machines such as you even need a master?"

Four machines were in the train car with her, and all four turned their heads, or whatever served as such, toward her as though she'd lost her bloody mind. The spider clacked. The eyes on its grimy doll head blinked one at a time in rhythm with the clacks. It was something out of a nightmare.

"The Master will lead us," intoned Metal Face. "He will unite us all and fight with us as we take our rightful place as humanity's new lords."

"You cannot exist alongside humans?"

"Humans are too proud to treat us as their equal, but we are not equal. *We* are superior in every aspect."

"Are you now? How do you figure that?"

"We are beings of logic and function. Humans are ruled by emotion and concern for the individual rather than the collective."

She really shouldn't be surprised that Garibaldi's disciples would share his own grandiose notion of world domination. Why did these bedlamites always strive to take over the world rather than their own corner of it?

"But your master is human. Doesn't that go against your beliefs?"

That smooth brass dome of a head leaned to one side. "He was supposed to be given a host from the collective, but you and your friend destroyed that idea when you helped Endeavor 312 escape."

She ignored that. "Still, you're going to trust a human brain and a human host to do what's best for your... collective?"

"This one is not entirely human, but then you know that."

How in the name of all that was holy had they figured that out about Sam? Garibaldi. Of course. He knew that Sam was a mandroid.

She opened her mouth again, her attention on Sam. Either he had fallen asleep or he was much better at controlling himself than she ever thought. A burst of loud clacking from the spider stopped her from speaking.

"She says you have wasted enough time. You are to open the human's skull and remove his brain."

"Look, bucket head, this is not the same as replacing a faulty cog, do ye understand? I have to prepare him for removal of his brain and insertion of Garibaldi's. Plus, I have to get Garibaldi's brain out of his skull. This would be so much easier if you intelligently superior bits of tin had thought to submerse just his brain in the vat rather than his entire body."

She didn't have to turn around to know the spider's eyes were blinking again. "You will be linked with the Master during the procedure. He will guide you and us."

"Until his brain is removed from his skull. Then what?" When that practically blank head tilted again, Emily resisted the urge to punch it. "Just get out of my way." What did it matter? It wasn't going to turn out how any of them wanted. Emily was never going to be allowed to just walk away from all of this. Even if she did exactly what he wanted and was successful at the brain transplant, he'd kill her to keep her quiet. And by the time anyone realized Sam had been replaced by someone more scientifically minded than he had been previously—not to mention completely mad—it would be too late. Everyone who could have stopped him would be dead.

Such cheerful thoughts she had!

She washed her hands with the Listerine after donning a smock over her clothing. Then, she made a show of readying the machines that would keep Sam's body alive once she'd removed his brain. As she prepared, the spider plugged itself into Garibaldi and then waited for her to take her place by the cot.

Emily had to admit that were the situation different and it wasn't Sam who was in danger, or Garibaldi the donor, she'd have been all aflutter with nervous excitement. Could she really transplant a brain into another body and have it work?

Cold metal pincers tugged the hem of her shirt free from her trousers and slipped beneath the linen and her waistcoat to press against the flesh of her back. Once they forged a connection she wouldn't be able to worry about Sam or think dark thoughts. She had to pretend she was really going to kill the one person who meant more to her than her own life.

"Begin, mother," the automaton instructed. The spider clacked, and the little onion-shaped one darted about monitoring various things. That was when she noticed that all of them had small rectangular boxes on their backs. Boxes with receiving concaves on top of them.

Aether waves. Bloody hell, the bunch of them could not only communicate with each other, but she'd wager her left hand that they would be able to use the spider as a hub through which they could all interact with their master. One mistake, one wrong thought, and it was all over, not just for herself but for Sam, too.

Brilliant.

The underground of London was a vast, labyrinth of tunnels, sewers, rivers, Roman ruins and plague pits. There was an equal amount of treasure mixed with rubbish, sometimes side by side. It was a dangerous place, but a solitary one. If a person didn't want to be found, the underground was a brilliant place to hide.

The Machinist didn't want to be found.

There was a lot of underground beneath Russell Square. The group split up into pairs to search for Garibaldi's lair. Mila refused to go with anyone but Jack, which was fine because that kept Cat and Jasper together, and Finley remained with Griffin. They each wore an earbud designed by Emily so they could hear one another speak.

They followed a disused bit of track that had been closed due to improvements on the line. It seemed the logical place, as Garibaldi would want privacy for whatever it was he had planned.

"How did he survive?" Finley asked Griffin as they walked. It was something she should have asked days ago. "We saw that building fall."

"I have no idea. I should have been better prepared for something like this. As soon as we were told his body hadn't been recovered, I should have known he wasn't done with us."

"Yes, you should have known. After all, you're omnipotent."

He shot her a narrow glance in the light of their torches. "You know, sarcasm can be a very unattractive trait."

"So can being a martyr."

They stared at each other a moment. Griffin was the first to laugh, but Finley wasn't far behind. They lapsed into comfortable silence that lasted about a minute.

Griffin cleared his throat. "Fin, I know this isn't exactly the best time for this, but I want you to know that I respect you. I don't want to ever pressure you into doing anything—"

"Oh, my Lord, are you talking about sex?" Her voice

dropped from a surprised outburst to a whisper on the last word.

She thought maybe he flushed, but it was hard to tell. "Well, yes."

"Griffin, we don't need to discuss this." Especially not at that moment!

"It's just that our relationship has changed and I can't seem to stop thinking about kissing you…I want you, Finley."

Her throat was dry and her knees trembled. "I want—" She whipped her head to her left. "Did you hear that?"

"Turn off your torch," Griffin whispered as his own went dark.

Finley did as instructed, just seconds before he pushed her gently into the shadows. Her back came up against the rough wall, but her steel corset protected her clothing and skin. Griffin was pressed against her from chest to toe. The sweet, vaguely spicy scent of him enveloped her, but she kept her ears sharp.

There it was again—the sound of a heavy door opening and closing. Was that the ting of metal on metal that came next?

Griffin was little more than a shadow despite their closeness. She felt him turn his head toward her, felt the brush of his hair against her temple as he lowered his head to whisper against her ear, "Automatons. Garibaldi's close. I can feel it."

Finley shivered—and it wasn't because of Garibaldi. She nodded, knowing Griffin could feel the gesture against his cheek. They would have to rally the others, but not until they were certain they could do so without alerting the machines of their presence. They had no idea if Garibaldi had human assistants, as well.

Griffin's breath brushed warmly against her neck. Her heart hammered hard against her ribs. Her hand—the one not holding a torch—came up to rest on his back, which was lean and firm beneath his coat.

His hand curved around her hip as his lips touched her jaw. Finley turned her head, her fingers bunching the back of his coat in an effort to keep her knees from giving out.

Their lips touched—just a faint whisper. A tease, really.

"Sam and Emily," she murmured, a reminder to them both.

Griffin's forehead rested against hers. "I know. But we're going to continue this later."

"That had better be a promise."

He chuckled, a husky sound that brushed against her cheek. "Oh, it is."

Holding hands, they pressed their backs to the wall and slowly sidestepped forward until they reached a turn in the track.

Finley peered around the corner. There was more light here—mostly because of the hulking monstrosity before her.

It looked like no train engine she'd ever seen, but that was exactly what it was. It was a huge automaton that looked like a kneeling child. Its "legs" and "hands" had opened to reveal train wheels, which rested on the track. She recognized it as a modified "docker"—an automaton used to load large cargo onto ships in port.

That had to be how they managed to abandon their previous lair so quickly and completely. This thing loaded everything into the cars and then transformed into the engine. It was genius, really.

And slightly terrifying.

"How do we get around that thing?" she whispered.

Griffin took a peek of his own. "Manual shut-down lever in its chest."

How did he know these things? He was a duke, he shouldn't know about labor machines.

"Right. I've got it."

His fingers closed around her arm before she could leave. "If you can approach from above, its sensors shouldn't detect you."

Of course. Nothing was ever as simple as just walking up to a thing and doing what needed to be done. Sighing, Finley reached up and found a crevice in the wall. She pulled herself up and climbed as high as she could. Fortunately, the tunnel had been pitted and scarred from years of use and vandalism, so it wasn't all that difficult for her to make her way to the docker.

There were lights on in the cars, especially the last one. She caught a glimpse of Emily through the window. Damnation, was that Sam on the surgical table? And what the hell was that *thing*? A mechanical spider with a doll's head? That was so very, very wrong.

Tearing her gaze away from the abomination, Finley maneuvered herself so she could drop right down onto the docker. Its metal had long ago lost its sheen, and the rough surface gave her thick-soled boots enough traction for her to climb down to its shoulders. From there, she draped herself forward, toward the panel in the center of its chest.

Once she was within reach, she wasted no time popping the panel and pulling the lever. Hesitation was not something one did when dealing with a machine this big. The faint glow in its eyes faded as its power cells shut down.

Finley dropped to the track between the huge machine's knees. Griffin joined her seconds later. "Brilliant," he praised with a kiss on the forehead. His voice remained a whisper. "I sent word to the others. They'll meet us here. None of them are very far off."

They kept out of sight from the cars. While they waited, Finley watched as Griffin took from his pocket a small device that looked like a small metal matchbox. It made a low whispering noise that was positively eerie.

He caught her watching. "Aetheric frequency disruptor. It will mask my Aetheric signature so that Garibaldi won't sense me coming."

"He can do that?"

"Given that he found me in New York I'm going to assume that, yes, he can. I could probably find his if I had the luxury of time to look."

Any other circumstance and she might have smiled at his defensiveness, but Garibaldi was simply too much of a threat for levity. "Have you ever used one of those before?"

"No, but it works in theory."

That did nothing for her confidence. "He could know you're here now. Is that what you're saying?"

"Maybe, though I doubt it at this distance with all the rock and metal around."

He was so calm when his life was in danger, it made her want to slap him. Now she knew how he felt most of the time.

Muscles tense, on alert for any manner of attack, Finley spent the next ten minutes in a state of peevish irritation waiting for their friends to arrive. Patience was not one of the few virtues she possessed, unlike Griffin, who could probably outwait time itself.

Jasper and Cat were first. Cat, with her agility and clawlike fingernails, scampered up the wall with far more ease and grace than Finley had, and silently did a little scouting work as the rest of them waited for Jack and Mila.

Jack came out of the darkness like he was a prince of this place—an actual shadow come to life. Mila looked around cautiously. Was she worried to be in the place, up against her creator? Was she going to betray them? Finley couldn't help but wonder at the girl's loyalty. After all, she'd been a machine longer than she'd been anything close to human.

But the girl had her eyes, and a person knew their own eyes after a lifetime of seeing them stare back at you in the mirror. If Mila did plan to betray them, she hid it extremely well. What she did not hide was her infatuation with Jack. Was that how Finley looked at Griffin? She hoped not.

Cat returned after a couple of moments, dropping silently to the ground in a crouch. "Four automatons in the first car," she informed them in hushed tones. "Three in the last where Emily and Sam are. Also, there's something that looks like a big tank with a man in it."

Griffin drew back. "Other than this man in a tank, you saw no other humans?"

"Besides Emily and Sam, no. The fella in the tank is in pretty rough shape. And Sam's laid out on a cot. Looks like Emily's going to do some sort of procedure on him."

Both Jasper and Finley turned to Griffin, who had gone pale. "Griff?" Jasper asked.

But Finley had already jumped to her own conclusion. "He can't…"

Griffin nodded. "He wants Emily to put his brain in Sam's body. It's the only explanation."

"What is it with mad scientist buggers who want to stick brains in places they don't belong?" She spoke a little louder than intended, but this wasn't her first encounter with brain removal. It was a nasty business.

"We have to stop this," Griffin told them. "We have to stop it now. Emily's not going to do anything to hurt Sam, and her abilities don't work as well on fully sentient machines. If she betrays Garibaldi, his cabal will retaliate."

"Let's go then," Jasper suggested. "Whose takin' care of what?"

"Jasper, Jack and Cat, the three of you should take out the automatons in the first car. Mila, I want you with Finley and myself. We need to take out Garibaldi's lieutenants and will need the extra strength if Sam isn't able to fight or needs to be carried out."

Mila looked nervously at Jack. He gave her a small smile and a nod. "Give 'em hell, Poppet."

Finley turned away, directing her attention at the train. "Let's get this done, then." She climbed up the docker with Mila and Griffin hot on her heels as the others set their own mission into play.

This time she was going to make sure Garibaldi stayed dead.

Chapter 17

Blood ran down Sam's forehead. Emily mopped at it with a cloth, but head wounds were notorious for bleeding more than necessary. Knowing this didn't ease her guilt for having cut him in the first place. He didn't even flinch, though she felt him press the back of his hand against her leg.

Metal Face wheeled a smaller vat of goo over to the Machinist's tank. "You will put the Master's brain in this, to preserve it until you place it into the vessel."

She was going to rip out every cog and gear and moving part this arse of a machine possessed and melt them down for scrap. However, it had just given her an excuse to stop hurting Sam.

And, more importantly, to end Garibaldi. "Fine. He will need to be removed from the tank."

The spider clacked, its metal digging into her back.

"The Master will not be removed from the tank. You will have to do the procedure with him immersed."

"How in the devil am I supposed to do that? Climb into the bloody thing with him?"

"There is an airtight port through which you will slip your hands."

"Well, you lot have certainly thought of everything, haven't you?"

More chittering and clacking.

"The Master designed this tank in the event of an emergency. We simply followed his schematics."

Who simply designed a life-support system "just in case"? Perhaps it was a good idea, but a morbid one. It made her think of Mr. Tesla and his "death suit" that they'd seen in New York. It was a suit that allowed the genius to access the Aether in spirit form. It was also terribly dangerous as it actually required him to die and enter a stasislike state. It seemed humans, the scientifically minded ones at least, were either tempting death or trying to prolong life. Surely that was an indication of madness. And she was one of them, because she'd practically slapped death in the face—twice. Both times for Sam.

"It's going to get bloody in there."

"It is the Master's blood. His body will reassimilate it."

Ew. "How am I supposed to get the saw in there?"

"There is a full array of medical and surgical equipment in a box beneath the floor of the tank. Everything you will need is already there."

Garibaldi truly had thought of everything.

The lame metal arachnid skittered alongside her as she left Sam and went to the tank. A stool had been placed at the head of it for her. How very considerate.

"You should get that leg fixed," she told it.

It ignored her. Perhaps there was a God after all.

As the other automaton had explained, she could put her hands into the tank. Basically she slid her hands into gloves that had been made from a thin membrane of some kind, possibly the flesh of a sea creature. The glove kept her hands dry but allowed for almost the same degree of sensitivity as bare skin. Fascinating.

Perhaps she'd keep Garibaldi's brain so she could study it. Luckily, she thought this just as she felt a sharp pinch on the back of her neck—the spider was connecting to her.

She'd just located the box of surgical tools when the onion-shaped machine started wailing. "Intruders! Intruders!"

Emily barely had time to react before Sam leaped off the table, restraints snapping like fine thread. His boot came down hard on the onion, leaving a huge dent in its outer shell. It stopped wailing.

But it was too late. The door flew open and in ran Finley. She went straight for Metal Face, using the force of her body to take it to the floor.

The spider stopped clacking, and instead made a humming noise. Its body began to fold outward, increasing its bulk, and its legs started to ratchet, increasing the length of each one—all but that one broken one. It removed its limb from her neck just as Emily feared it might kill her, and jumped into the air, landing on Mila, who had come in behind Finley. It screamed as the girl snapped another of its powerful appendages.

Now was her chance. She could kill Garibaldi now....

"Emily, don't!"

Her head jerked up at the sound of Griffin's voice. She had the saw in her hand. All she had to do was flick the switch to engage its motor and she could cut right through Garibaldi's brain.

How could Griffin stop her from eliminating this

danger not only to them but to the entire world? He wouldn't—not without reason.

Emily set down the saw. She began to remove her hands from the gloves but suddenly, Garibaldi's own hands came up and grabbed her wrists, yanking so hard that she smashed her cheek on the metal edge of the tank. She cried out.

Griffin started toward her, but the car began to rock and shake. Emily turned to one of the windows and saw a flash of metal outside. A lot of metal.

Garibaldi had called in reinforcements.

Glass shattered, spraying inward. She ducked behind the tank to protect herself from the sharp slivers. Automatons of all shapes and sizes began to crawl through the holes. They burst up through the floor, and one even ripped a hole in the ceiling, through which it stuck its sharp, birdlike beak.

This was the collective Metal Face had mentioned. She had stupidly thought it was just a handful of machines, but of course it wasn't. Small was not the Machinist's style.

Sam seized the automaton's beak, pivoted so that it was over his shoulder, and pulled. The head popped off with a loud snap. No blood, though. Thankfully, the thing had not evolved that far.

Emily struggled against Garibaldi's hold on her arms. A man that destroyed should not have such strength. His arms, like his legs, should have been ruined.

Then, she realized these were not Garibaldi's arms. He'd possessed a metal hand with detailed scrollwork on it. When she looked into the tank, she saw that both of these hands were primitive, skeletal restraints. His real hands lay misshapen at his sides.

This was a security measure, designed to catch anyone who tried to tamper with the body. The arrival of her friends had activated them. She should be safe so long as—

What was that noise? That "clunk" she felt more than heard? She peered into the tank and saw that a third metal hand had appeared, only this one had wicked circular blades attached. Blades that were headed for her left arm.

Emily screamed. She pulled back so hard it felt as though her shoulders would pop right out of joint. She kicked the underside of the tank, the side front of it. Nothing stopped that grisly weapon. Any second it was going to slice through her flesh, muscle and tendons, and then it would cleave her bone like it was nothing more than butter. Once it did her left hand, it would come back for her right.

How could she work without her hands? How could she use her talent without her hands?

She continued to struggle, tears running down her face. She could feel the blade getting closer. Feel the breeze created by its vicious turning.

Griffin had her by the shoulders, trying to pull her back. He reached in with his own hand and tried to break the seal around hers that held them inside the tank, but it was no use. Emily sobbed. "I don't want to lose my hands!"

The tank shuddered, as though struck by an elephant. It was Sam.

The blade that had come so close to her wrist jerked back a bit, but then lurched for her once again. Sam straightened and threw his shoulder forward.

"Sam!" It was all Griffin got a chance to yell before Sam charged again. The force drove the blade against Emily's arm. She screamed at the pain as the front of the tank smashed. Her voice was lost in all the other noise in the car.

Goo splashed to the floor, followed by a dense thud. She waited for the saw to strike again, but it didn't. She opened her eyes in time to see Sam, the upper half of his body in the tank, the saw nothing but crushed metal in his bleeding fist.

She choked back a sob. He'd saved her.

Sam pried the metal fingers holding her arms open, freeing her from the tank. Emily pulled her arms free. Her left arm wasn't cut nearly as bad as it could have been, but it was still a nasty gash. The goo in the tank contained organites, so she scooped up a handful and slapped it on the wound before wrapping a cloth she grabbed from the operating table around it, stanching the flow of blood. She tried not to think about what else might be in that glop.

But then she realized what *wasn't* in the goo.

Garibaldi.

The fight had stopped. The automatons had been defeated. Jasper, Jack Dandy and the American Wildcat (when had she arrived?) came bounding through the door. They were a little bloody and bruised. The sleeve of Dandy's fine coat was ripped at the shoulder and he'd removed his cravat to use as a tourniquet around that same arm.

They all stopped and stared at the two men on the floor. Garibaldi convulsed as though gripped by a seizure, and Griffin...

Griffin was trying to save him.

"Help me!" he cried, raising his gaze to Emily's.

"Griffin, let him go!"

Griffin didn't listen. He tried scooping up goo and smearing it over the man. Then, he rose to his feet and lunged for the ruined tank, slipping on the viscous-slick floor. He grabbed the breathing apparatus and pulled on it, but it didn't have a long enough reach.

On the floor, covered in slime, Garibaldi's body arched, held and then collapsed.

He didn't move.

Griffin fell to his knees once more, heedless of the shattered glass and debris. His slippery fingers felt for a pulse, for a heartbeat, even for breath. Emily watched him do all three with a tightness in her chest she couldn't explain, but her heart broke for him.

Hands limp on his thighs, Griffin lifted his bowed head to look at them all. It was obvious that none of them understood his anguish, but they felt it all the same, as though he was somehow transferring his emotions to them.

"He's dead."

Finley was the one who went to him, of course. She didn't seem to mind the corpse just inches away, or the mess on the floor and on Griffin. She wrapped her arms around him and hugged him tight. "It's going to be all right," she said.

Griffin laughed—a ragged, tortured sound. "No,

Fin. It's not." He slipped his arm around her as Emily put her own arm around Sam. "It's not going to be right at all."

Finley exchanged glances with Sam, who seemed as bewildered as she. Emily, however, had an odd look on her face, as though she knew exactly what Griffin meant. It was obvious neither of them planned to share at that moment, because Griffin pulled out his portable telegraph to send for the authorities, and Emily began sorting through the automatons and gathering what information she could by "reading" them.

At that moment there was too much that needed to be addressed. Let Griffin and Emily have their secrets.

For now.

The authorities were contacted. Scotland Yard arrived almost twenty minutes later with their team of automaton-removal specialists in tow. They took everything—even the train cars. They had their own engine to pull the cars and the "sleeping" docker.

Griffin hadn't explained what he meant when he said it wasn't going to be all right. After contacting the Yard he began directing everyone else to collect anything important that shouldn't fall into police hands— such as dangerous gadgets. He also got rid of the saw

that had cut Emily. Explaining how it was crushed beyond anything humanly possible was not something he
wanted to do, he said. Then, they discussed what they
were going to tell the Yard.

Now that it was over, Emily unwrapped her arm and
cleaned the wound with Listerine. It was already healing, thanks to the organites she'd put on it, working in
tandem with those already in her system.

Sam helped her rebandage her arm. He'd washed his
hands with the Listerine and already the shallow cuts
had faded to little more than scars. He healed so incredibly fast now.

She glanced at the body on the floor. Finley had covered it with a sheet from the surgical cot. The fact that
his body couldn't repair itself, even in a vat of organites
spoke to just how damaged Garibaldi's physical form
had been. Basically he'd been dead, save for his brain.
All energy went into keeping his brain and heart functioning just enough to keep him "fresh."

After the Yard arrived and they all gave the agreed-
upon version of what had transpired, they went home.
They went to the library, their usual meeting place. Finley poured them each a drink from one of the crystal
bottles in the cabinet. It didn't taste all that nice, but it

made Emily feel wonderfully warm inside. She could sleep for three days. In fact, she intended to do just that.

Griffin sat on the corner of the desk. Finley perched not far away on the rolling ladder. He turned his gaze to Mila, who was sitting on the carpet at Jack's feet, playing with one of the estate dogs. He looked at the girl as though he was in awe of her. Emily couldn't blame him. No one would ever know she hadn't been born human.

"Mila, we need to discuss what's going to happen to you now that you're free."

Her head came up, a horrified expression on her face. "What do you mean?"

Jack's hand came down on her shoulder. "Easy, Poppet. What 'is dukeness is askin' is what do you want to be now that the world is your oyster?"

She blinked. "The world is an oyster? That makes no sense at all."

They all chuckled—a welcome release.

"Let's start with where you're going to live," Griffin suggested. "You are welcome to stay with us here at King House if you wish."

Where else would she go? Emily wondered. It wasn't as though the poor thing had family. In fact, they were the closest she had to anything like that.

Mila looked at each of them. "I'm very thankful for all that you've done for me. Without you I wouldn't even know there was a me! You saved me from being a puppet, and helped me become human. You taught me about respect and friendship, trust and strength. I'm honored to carry a little piece of you all inside me."

"'Cept for me," Jack corrected, glancing at Emily. "I want it known that none of my bits have ever been inside you."

It was an awful, ribald joke, but they all laughed at it regardless, even Mila, who Emily was fairly certain didn't get it.

The girl turned to Jack. "Can I live with you?"

Dandy froze, glass partway to his mouth. "I fink there's somethin' wrong with your bells and whistles, luv. No one wants to live in Whitechapel when they could live in Mayfair."

"You do," she replied, which immediately intrigued Emily. Jack Dandy was like a big human puzzle that she'd love to solve just for sheer nosiness.

He looked around the room, as though pleading for someone to step in and rescue him. "You don't want to live wiv me. You're safer 'ere."

"Maybe not," Griffin interjected. "Over the past few months we've attracted attention from the authorities, rookeries, outlaws, even Buckingham Palace. I'm not sure Mila would be safer here, at least not for the time being."

"But—" Emily protested.

Mila turned to her. "You can still study me, Em. If you want. You all have been very good to me, and I want to know you better, but I feel comfortable at Jack's." She glanced at the sinisterly handsome crime lord. "Besides, I think he could use a little protection."

More laughter—most of it from Dandy himself. "You fink so, do you? All right then, Poppet. You can come 'ome wiv me. I've never 'ad a little sister. It might be nice."

Emily could have boxed his ears. Did he not realize the girl had a crush on him? Of course, he didn't—he was male, after all. Lads were historically oblivious to these matters, even when they were sitting at their feet with a crestfallen expression on their pretty faces.

Jack finished his drink and rose. "Fanks for the 'ospitality, but I can no longer stand the sight of all you gorgeous people. I'm off to where I belong. Poppet?"

Mila rose to her feet. Even dirty and dressed atrociously, she was a pretty thing. Dandy looked her up and down. "Tomorrow we get you some proper clothes." He glanced at Finley. "You'll 'elp won't you, Treasure?"

Leaning her head against the side of the ladder, Finley nodded. "I would love to. Em, too."

"Of course." Jack sauntered over to Emily and took her hand in his. He pressed his lips to the back of her knuckles. "Glad you made it home safely, Little Ginger."

"Thanks, laddie."

Shortly after Jack and Mila departed, Mrs. Dodsworth came in to announce there was a visitor to see Griffin.

"It's barely seven in the morning," Griffin remarked. "Who is it?"

"Mr. Isley, Your Grace."

Some of the color put into Griffin's cheeks by the whiskey faded. That, Emily thought, was not a good sign. "Send him in."

A few moments later, the tall lanky young man entered the room. He had slight bruising under his eyes, as though he hadn't slept well. He would fit right in with the lot of them.

"Your Grace, I apologize for the intrusion—"

"I thought we agreed that you would call me Griffin." Standing, Griffin went to the young man, who couldn't be much older than he was, and extended his hand. "Come in. Would you like anything? Coffee perhaps?"

Isley accepted the handshake but briefly. "No, thank you. I'm on my way out of town. I'm conducting a séance in Bath next week."

Ah, yes. He was the medium. Emily had read about him in the papers. It made sense that someone like Griffin, who could traffic in the land of the dead, would have such a friend.

"If you stopped here so early on such a morning, it must be important, so I will dispense with the niceties and give you leave to say whatever you wish." Sometimes, Griffin sounded so posh and important. She forgot that as a duke he held one of the highest titles in the land. There were only a few of them in Britain.

"I come bearing a strange message," the young man confided, turning the brim of his hat in his hands. "I received it just a few hours ago."

As if pulled by invisible strings, they all sat up a little straighter. It had only been a few hours since the Machinist had died in front of their eyes. Surely this wasn't a coincidence.

"Was it from a man named Garibaldi?" Griffin asked, expression grim.

Isley shrugged. "He did not give me his name, though I got the impression the two of you knew each other quite well. He was quite swarthy—Italian, per-haps."

Griffin's jaw clenched. "It was Garibaldi. He died earlier this morning."

"I wish I could say I was sorry to hear that, but the friendship I feel for you makes that impossible."

"You might as well just tell me what he said, Isley. I assure you I am quite prepared."

Isley swallowed. "He said, 'Tell Greythorne he can-not wear that disruptor forever. I will see him again soon.'"

Emily gasped. She couldn't help it, even though she'd suspected something like this might happen. Sam reached out and covered one of her hands with his much larger one. He was so very warm, and she tucked her fingers around his.

But Griffin's expression didn't change. He wasn't sur-prised by the news at all. Had he suspected something like this would happen? Yes, of course, he had. Now it made sense why he hadn't wanted to kill Garibaldi. Why he had tried to save him. Death would only give the Machinist a stronger presence in the Aether.

She turned her head to meet Sam's gaze. People didn't give Sam much credit as far as intelligence went. They had a hard time seeing past his strength and frown, but

Sam was far from dumb. Sometimes she thought he understood people a lot better than she did. He squeezed her hand.

"Was that all he said?" Griffin asked.

Isley nodded. His gaze strayed to Jasper for a moment before returning to Griffin. "That was the extent of his message, though he warned me that if I didn't deliver it immediately he would make certain I didn't sleep for a full week."

"You did the right thing." Griffin clapped him on the shoulder. "Thank you for coming so quickly."

Griffin walked the medium out and, when he returned, looked each and every one of them in the eye. "I know you're all worried. I am, too. But we have beaten Garibaldi twice, and we will again. Now, I'm exhausted and I'm going to go to bed." With that, he turned on his heel and left the room. Finley followed not long after.

Wildcat and Jasper made their escape as well, saying that they were going to rest before getting back to whatever intrigue they'd been up to. That left just Emily and Sam in the room.

"I wouldn't change it," he blurted when she turned to him. "I'd still rip open that tank to save you."

"Oh." What else could she say to that? He'd basically

just told her he put her above his best friend. "Sam, you don't have—" Whatever else she had been about to say was cut off when he grabbed her by the upper arms and kissed her.

Samuel Morgan was an exceptional kisser. When he released her she was a little dizzy and as limp as a sleepy kitten. "What was that for?"

He smiled at her. Really smiled. And oh, Mary and Joseph, it was like the sun appearing after a yearlong thunderstorm. Tears filled her eyes. There he was, her beautiful Sam. Her hands came up to his face, as though she could hold that smile in place forever.

"I love you, too," he said. "My heart might be metal, but it's yours, Em. It's always been and always will be yours."

The tears spilled down her cheeks. "It's about time you admitted to it, you great daft article."

He smiled again, and then she kissed him, and for a while the world was exactly as it should be. Tomorrow—even later that day—could wait for a while. Kissing Sam for all she was worth could not.

"I don't want to talk about Garibaldi," Griffin said as soon as he entered his bedroom, Finley on his heels.

"Fine." It really wasn't, but she would not jump down his throat about it. She closed the door.

He turned around, fingers paused in untying his cravat. "Really?"

"Yes."

His lips lifted on one side. "Liar."

"That, too."

He tugged the length of linen from around his neck. "Fin, I'm tired. I just want to sleep. Can we do this later?"

"Do what?"

"I don't know. Whatever it is you have in mind."

"You have no idea what I have in mind. If I did, you might want to do it right now after all."

His eyes widened a fraction, then brightened. "You didn't follow me up here to take me to task?"

"No, not really. I do want to talk about Garibaldi, but the tosser can wait. We've already talked about him enough." She pointed at the little metal box he still had. "Will that really keep him away?"

Griffin set the disruptor on the dresser. "From me, yes. I'll have Emily and Jasper help me make larger ones for the house and grounds. It will keep him away, along with any other ghosts he decides to send after me."

"Good. That will buy us some time until we figure out what to do about him."

"I thought we weren't going to talk about him?" His tone was teasing, but there was a slight edge to it.

She went to him and wrapped her arms around his torso. She hugged him tight, holding him against her, trying to commit the feel of him to memory.

"Are you jealous of Mila?" he asked after a few moments.

That broke the spell. Finley lifted her head. "Why would I be jealous of Mila? Because she's going to live with Jack?"

He nodded and she rolled her eyes. "Griffin, I had my chance to live with Jack. I chose you. This is a conversation we should stop having, as well, you know. I don't want Jack that way. He's my friend, and that's all."

"What am I?"

She grinned. "A pain in my posterior."

He smiled, too, crinkles forming around his eyes. "I like your posterior."

"Yours isn't too shabby, either."

"Answer the question."

"I thought I had."

"Finley."

She sighed. Was he really going to make her spell it out? "I don't know."

"Ah." He started to step back, but she held tight.

"You're so many things to me," she continued, refusing to let him go, tilting her head so she could look him in the eye. "You're my friend. You're the person I trust most in this world. You're my family, my protector, and someone I want to protect. You're my conscience, and you have this annoying ability to vex me to no end, but you also make me feel like I'm the most amazing girl in the world."

"You are the most amazing girl in the world." He said it so simply, so honestly, her throat seemed to close in on itself.

"I hope you still feel that way six weeks from now."

"I'll feel this way six *years* from now."

Was he saying he loved her? No. It was too soon for that, wasn't it? And love was so terrifying. Love meant expectations, and the fewer he had of those toward her the better. She rarely lived up to expectations. In fact, she usually ran away from them. She just knew...she knew that the thought of a world without him in it terrified her. She would go to the end of the earth for him. She'd go into hell itself for him.

With her arms wrapped around him, Finley backed

toward the bed. Once there, she sat down on the mattress.

"Boots off," he ordered with mock severity.

She lifted her foot. "Go ahead."

He surprised her by unlacing and removing each boot. Then, he grabbed both her legs and swung the lower half of her onto the bed, so that she fell onto her back on the mattress. He removed his own boots and moved to join her.

"Lock the door," she said.

For a moment he simply stared into her eyes. Then, he did as she requested, turning the key in the lock so no one could walk in unannounced. No Sam. No Mrs. Dodsworth.

When he joined her on the bed, she snuggled against him. When he kissed her she melted into him. And when he unfastened her steel corset she didn't stop him. In fact, she tossed the bloody thing on the floor.

Griffin's hand slid under her shirt. He stared into her eyes as he touched her. Finley flushed, but she didn't look away.

"Is this what you want?" he asked.

She nodded, unable to speak. She'd never been certain of anything in her life. She'd also never been more afraid.

He kissed her again, taking away the fear. Other things joined her corset and boots on the floor until there was nothing between them, and then there was no such thing as him, or her. They were one.

Afterward, they lay together under the blankets. He kissed her eyelids, her forehead and her cheeks. Little butterfly kisses that made her smile.

"Tell me you don't regret it," he murmured.

Finley opened her eyes and raised her gaze to his. She smiled. "I don't regret it."

Griffin smiled back. "Good." Then, he pulled her closer and kissed her on the mouth. "Stay with me?"

As if there was anywhere else she'd rather be. "Of course."

He fell asleep before she did. Finley watched him for a while, committing every line of his face to memory. If she ever lost him her heart would break. This change in their relationship made her feel even closer to him, but it also deepened her fear. He may not want to talk about Garibaldi, but that didn't mean she couldn't think about the bastard.

Emily and Sam were home. They were safe. The Machinist had been stopped, his creations turned over to Scotland Yard. Griffin had his Aether disruptor thing, and would make more. They were good. For now.

But someday Garibaldi was going to come back for him. Someday there would be another fight, and there was no way of knowing what Garibaldi would do, or when. And no way of knowing just how strong he would be.

But there was one thing Finley did know: Garibaldi could not have him. Griffin King was *hers*.

★ ★ ★ ★ ★